Fishing for Hyenas & looking for sleeping Penguins

A story of my
BIG 5 HOLIDAY ADVENTURES

John CT Miller

Fishing for Hyenas and Looking for Sleeping Penguins

Copyright 2014 John CT Miller

Published by Piggle Design

The moral rights of the author have been affirmed
and all rights reserved.

Condition of Sale
This book is sold subject to the condition that it shall not, by way of
trade or otherwise, be lent, re-sold, hired out or otherwise circulated in
any form of binding or cover other than that in which it is published
and without a similar condition including this condition being imposed
on the subsequent purchaser.

Disclaimer
This book is a work of fiction. Names, places, characters, and events are
the product of the author's imagination. Any resemblance to actual per-
sons, living or dead, events, or locales is purely coincidental.

ISBN: 978-0-9927934-8-7

John CT Miller is a former South African journalist, who previously covered and wrote about entertainment, courts, crime, and consumer affairs, before settling in the UK and turning his hand to writing books.

Journey 1

Heading South and looking for sleeping penguins

Day 1

"This is your captain speaking: Welcome to O.R. Tambo airport Johannesburg. The temperature on the ground is currently 18c. Now that the safest part of your journey is over, may I wish you a safe trip further."

Helen my English borne partner had during the preceding years heard a lot from me about South Africa; now with me, the self appointed guide to the country I loved, and through her own experiences was about to find out how true my observations were.

Since living in the UK for over a decade, I had told her almost daily how great the country was, how great its people were, how great the wildlife was and how great the local cuisine was.

Unfortunately, she had also heard and read about the high levels of violent crime, the highjackings, murders, and rapes in and around Johannesburg and the rest of the country.

I don't think the joke from the pilot on landing helped to quell her apprehension.

Shortly before we left the UK, there had been a series of highjackings in Johannesburg, and these had left her feeling a bit on edge.

His words didn't help her sense of anticipation and excitement. A new country, new sights, just waiting to be enjoyed, and may be as far as she was concerned just waiting to be high jacked.

I tried to reassure her, the message from the pilot was a joke, and part of our sense of humour.

"Remember Penguin, we are not going on the Johannesburg highways and we will only be in transit for a couple of hours before we catch our next flight to Cape Town." I said.

About 2 hours later, the world famous Table Mountain came briefly in to view as we flew over it on our way to land. This time there were no jokes from the cockpit.

The Mountain as it is called by locals stands 1,084m looking over the city, and is flanked on either side by Devil's Peak to the east, and Lion's Head to the west.

It wouldn't be long before Helen would find out for her self how right I was about all things South African.

As we circled over Cape Town, ready to land, Helen got her first view of townships, squatter camps, big houses with big fenced in yards and many with swimming pools.

"I can't believe the wealth and on the other hand the poverty." She said.

For years Helen had heard so much about all the wonderful things in the country: braais (barbecues), boerewors (a spicy farm sausage), biltong (wind dried strips of meat), pap (a maize meal thick porridge), similar to polenta, koeksisters (a South African syrup-coated type doughnut.) The Afrikaner version is a twisted or braided shape, while the Cape Malay version is a spicy treat finished off with a sprinkling of coconut, and don't forget milktert, which is similar to a custard tart, but better.

During our yearly visits or once again as she now calls it "pilgrimage", she would be taken in each time by the sights, the friendliness and generosity of the people, the wildlife and not forgetting the food.

While she looked forward to each new sight, I looked forward to the biltong, the steaks, the warmth of the people and good old traditional South African food.

Perhaps I should mention at this stage that we are both animal and in particular dog lovers, and we got to meet and know many four-legged friends through out the country.

Before you get to meet them, let me return to that first trip.

I had decided in order to give Helen the true South African experience, we would fly South African Airways, which any self respecting compatriot would do.

In a previous life, I had been an aviation journalist, and flew many times both locally and internationally with SAA.

It was an airline to be proud of. SAA pilots have been recognised around the world as the best, and the cabin crew extremely professional.

The trip started badly. There was a delay at Heathrow. We and other passengers sat for almost one hour, not knowing why or what had caused the delay.

My patience finally ran out, and I got up from my seat and went in search of any flight attendant.

"What is happening?" I demanded to know.

"I'm not sure myself." The reply came from one of the cabin crew.

"Well, the least you could do is to let the passengers know why there is a delay, and if you don't know ask the captain, who can tell the passengers." I said in an exasperated tone.

Shortly after the one on one encounter with a member of the cabin crew, an announcement was finally made explaining the delay.

This was not the end of the many problems that evening. The flight crew had forgotten to pack passenger headsets.

While it might not be that much of an inconvenience to many of the passengers, but to me, a blind person, it did create a slight problem. Silent movies were no good to me.

I might sound like a winging pom, but I reject this accusation. All I wanted was Helen to have a great time flying with SAA, and that the flight would be a prelude to all the wonderful things I had planned for Helen during the next 14 days.

Unfortunately, thanks to affirmative action, in-flight standards on SAA have dropped.

One of the old-timer flight attendants, who I spoke to on the flight out to Johannesburg agreed with me, and blamed the situation on affirmative action. He told me he was only staying on with the airline simply to get his pension.

"I am a white middle aged male, and with affirmative action, stand no chance of getting promotion let alone ever finding another job if I leave.

I know standards have dropped, but as long as I keep my head down and watch my back, I'll be alright. Anyway, only 3 more years to go." He told me later that night.

I had also forgotten that on a long hall flight Helen spent most of the hours watching movies, and didn't like to be interrupted.

The best way of attracting her attention was to poke her in the ribs. This would be followed by a "what do you want" or "what do you want now?"

Watching movies was her form of relaxing, and passing the time.

The sooner this flight is forgotten the better. When we landed at O.R. Tambo airport in Johannesburg the next day, we were greeted by and helped by some lovely people. Well done (AcSA), the Airports Company of South Africa.

"Wow, it is great to be back home." I said to Helen. I had missed the warm and friendly tones of the black African accents.

As we were guided through the airport, I secretly hoped Helen was taking notice how friendly people were, unlike the often stuffy and formal attitude adopted by British officials.

One other concern for Helen was that she had only been driving for about 2 years, and this would be the first time to drive in a foreign country, let alone the apparent total disregard for traffic rules shown by most local motorists.

After a brief stop-over in Johannesburg we took off for Cape Town. "Not long to go" I said to Helen.

On arriving at Cape Town International Airport my beating of the drum on behalf of South Africa was momentary silenced.

When we collected our luggage, Helen noticed that her suitcase had been broken in to.

"So much for you telling me how great things are" Helen muttered.

No problems to the staff at the airport. Simply fill in a form, take your suitcase to one of 3 outlets in the city, and if they couldn't fix it, would replace it.

Before she had time to voice her further displeasure, I sprang to my defence.

"Helen, I know someone has broken in to your suitcase, but look at the good service we are getting from the airport? I bet we wouldn't get such quick and great service any where else."

Although we had been told it was a fairly common occurrence, hence the swift action to have the case either mended or replaced their concern and help was still much appreciated.

After collecting the hire car, and putting the broken suitcase along with my intact suitcase in the boot, off we drove in the direction of Camps Bay, one of the well heeled suburbs to find our first guest house.

My duties as a guide were about to begin. I was going to share her experiences through her eyes, and in return, she would enjoy many of the sites through my knowledge of the country.

The temperature that January afternoon was 27°c and during the next 5 days as we traveled through the Cape would climb to almost 40°c.

"Penguin, are you ready to leave and start the journey? I asked as she started the car.

"Well ready as I am ever going to be" she said in an apprehensive tone.

After a nervous start, it didn't take Helen long to decide she was now used to driving in South Africa, and thanks to our satnav, we drove straight to the guest house.

Our first hosts were Bonnie and Clide, and they were

not the infamous gangster couple, and yes it was their real names.

When we got there, and after introductions, we had a brief chat with Bonnie and Clide. We or rather I, talked about the state of the country, and then were also introduced to Marko, their elderly deaf corgi.

The swimming pool on the patio outside our bedroom looked inviting, so we decided to have a dip.

It is hard to believe, that Camps Bay with its white sandy beaches now lined with palm trees was once inhabited by the San people, and the 12 Apostles were covered in forests with lion, leopard and antelope roaming freely. It soon became a favourite hunting ground for some of the British settlers.

This holiday, which Helen or as I lovingly called her "Penguin" for the past 10 years would describe it as a "Military manoeuvre" had begun.

We had 14 days to cover and see and experience as much as was possible.

During the previous few months I had drawn up a list of things to do and places to visit each day.

Helen, my special Penguin is a list person. Each Friday night she wanted a list of things that needed to do over the weekend. If not emailed to her by 5pm she would ask "where's my list?"

She had printed out our itinerary before leaving. The schedule included a day by day list of things to do, where we would be staying, places to visit, approximate distances between towns, important telephone numbers bank and credit card details as well as various emergency numbers.

There was also another list with places to eat.

After our swim I said to Helen, "I think we had better go up Table Mountain this afternoon."

My suggestion was received with what can best be described as a Luke warm reception.

"Do we have to go, and could we not go up tomorrow? I've hardly slept a wink for the past 36 hours."

I quickly said "No, No.

You never know, the cable way could be closed because of bad weather, so it's better if we do it while the going is good and if you are lucky, you will get to see, what Capetonians call the white table cloth, when the clouds slowly make their way over and down the mountain.

This happens when the south-easterly winds blow, and I don't know what the weather will be like tomorrow."

Helen sighed and with a resigned tone said "well, if you really think so, I guess we had better go".

As we got in the car and locked the doors, Helen jokingly said

"Are all South African dogs disabled or did they get this one especially for you?

Not only will I have to look after a blind person, but a deaf dog as well."

We were fortunate not to have to wait long in line at the bottom cable station, having previously booked and paid in the UK for our trip up the famous mountain.

While on the subject of the internet, all our accommodation had been researched and booked before we left.

In most cases, what you saw and what you read was correct, but in some cases, the accommodation and facilities were not always what they were made out to be.

Once we boarded the cable car and as it made its way up to the top of the mountain slowly spinning a full 360 degrees it was not just Helen I could hear with numerous "wow" and "look there!!" But similar echoes of wonder and delight from the other visitors.

Reaching the top station, we all stepped out of the car, and made our way around the top of the mountain with the sounds of excited tourists in front and behind us.

"Wow! Helen said I can see Camps Bay, Robben Island, the new soccer stadium, and so much more."

Some locals, who heard us talking came across and pointed out other sights which could be seen from our vantage point.

She also got her first view of Fynbos, a mixture of heath, Protea, Iris, aloes and geranium plants, which can be found around many parts of the southern and south Western Cape.

The name Fynbos comes from the Dutch meaning fine-leaved plants.

Fynbos forms part of the Cape Floral Kingdom, one of only 6 floristic kingdoms in the world. This kingdom, the smallest of its kind stretches from Klein William to near Port Elizabeth along the Garden Route.

Another unique feature of these plants is they need fire to germinate and spread.

Having viewed the sites below from different vantage points, we grabbed a quick refreshment, before making our way back to the cable station, to begin our descent down the mountain. On our way down, between more ""wow!!" And "look at that, look over there" from Helen and the other tourists she caught sight of a dassie as it is known or rock rabbit.

The day was not yet over, and we drove to one of the Camps Bay beaches.

We parked the car, and she got to meet her first of many car guards. These guards are found throughout the country and will suddenly appear as you are about to park your vehicle.

They will meet and greet you as you step out of your car, and for a small fee will offer to look after the car until you return.

It is then expected you will tip them for having looked after your car while you were away.

We walked along the beach chatting about our first few hours in the city.

I was eager to find out what Helen thought.

With the sound of waves on one side, and on the other the sound of children playing, I asked "so what do you think Penguin? Are you enjoying your self? Is this what you expected?"

I had many more questions, but these were enough to start with.

"Even though I am tired, it is wonderful. I love the warm and clear air, how relaxed and laid back people seem to be. I know you have told me all this before, but until anyone is actually here, it is difficult to really appreciate everything" she said with a smile in her voice.

Before I could reply she said "hey look, there's a Nando's. Shall we go and get something to eat from there?"

In the UK we had been to Nando's a couple of times, but this would be different. A Nando's meal in the country where it all started in Johannesburg in 1987.

This restaurant chain of over 1000 outlets in 24 countries world wide offers Portuguese Mozambican peri-peri flame grilled chicken.

The company has also become well known for its controversial and humorous adverts, many of which can be viewed on You Tube.

Part of getting to know South Africa was taking Helen to not only up market restaurants, but also eating at several of the restaurants many South Africans had grown up with.

"I guess we might as well. It is one of the restaurants on your places to eat list" I said.

As we waited for our order of hot peri-peri chicken with salad, Helen was able to look out over the beach and at the sea.

"I'm so happy" she said.

"You mean flying all this way to eat at Nando's makes you happy?" I said mockingly.

After the meal, we made our way via Pick n Pay to buy a few yoghurts before returning happy and contented to the guest house.

Once we got back, we went for another swim, and Marko came to visit us again: sitting on the edge of the pool watching over us.

He remained with us while we sat and sipped a glass of wine.

Our hosts like all those to come on this and other trips were quick to say "just ignore our dogs".

Naturally we did not listen, but instead ignored the advice of the owners.

I am sure that dogs have a sixth sense and somehow know if the new arrival is a dog lover or not.

This was always the case at almost every guest house we stayed at. The dogs would come to us, and most times remain with us until we went out for the day.

Now you might say it has something to do with the biltong I had with me, but I think you might be wrong, or so I hope.

Each time we landed in South Africa, I would make sure I had some biltong waiting at the guest house, or would stop en route to buy some biltong.

Needless to say, after making our way inside, we were both fast a sleep as soon as our heads touched the pillow.

Day 2

There had been so many firsts for Helen the previous day. Her first trip to the Southern hemisphere, the first to South Africa, her first time to drive on South African roads and to crown it all, a trip up Table Mountain.

One of the many bird calls I miss and look forward to hearing is the Ibis, or as it is known in South Africa the Hadeda.

The Hadeda has a loud and distinctive call and can be heard first thing in the morning, and at times during the day, and once again in the evening.

This large bird is grey-to-partly brown in colour and has a narrow, white, roughly horizontal stripe across its cheeks. The feathers over the wings have a shiny purple sheen. The bird has blackish legs and a large grey-to-black bill with a red stripe on the upper mandible. Part of the toes are also red.

Every time we return to South Africa and each morning I hear the Hadeda I rejoice in being back. That loud call for me is very much part of South Africa.

While the sound of the Red-chested Cuckoo or as it is commonly known in the country the piet-my-vrou due to the sound of its call, as well as the go-away bird or Grey Lourie remind me of Africa, they can't beat the call of the Hadeda and its significance, and appeal it has to me.

When we opened the door the next morning, Marko was outside our door to greet us, while we enjoyed our breakfast of yogurt on the patio. It was time to explore Cape Town, but not before Marko enjoyed a bit of biltong.

Today we would visit Hout Bay, Simons Town and the Cape Point lighthouse.

"Come on Helen, it's time to show you more of the country."

This time my suggestion was not greeted with a sigh.

"How are you feeling today?" I asked.

"I'm feeling fine. I needed that sleep. So let's see what your country has to offer today" she said.

Our first stop later that morning was Mariner's Wharf in Hout Bay to sample their various fish dishes.

After leaving Camps Bay, we took the coastal road via Llandudno and into Hout Bay.

When we arrived at the restaurant, we were fortunate to get a table outside on the deck overlooking the bay.

Drinks taken care of, it was time to look at the menu.

I waited a while before asking Helen "anything you fancy?"

Silence for a while before she said "there are so many things I would like to try but..."

"But what?"

"I don't know what to have."

"If you tell me what's on the menu, I might be able to suggest something."

After Helen read through the menu, I asked once again

"What do you think you might have?"

Our deliberations were interrupted when a smartly dressed waiter appeared and asked "are you ready to order?"

"No, we haven't decided yet, can you give us a couple of minutes?

So Penguin, back to what you fancy."

"Well, you know how I love avo? They have this Avocado Bounty overflowing with shrimp, but I also like the sound of these other dishes like Wharfside Salad with chargrilled chicken with roasted almonds and pineapple mayonnaise, and Regatta Salad with smoked salmon, avocado and feta cheese.

What are you going to have?"

"You must be joking!! Chicken at a seafood restaurant?"

"What do you mean?"

"Don't tell me you are thinking of having the chicken at a seafood restaurant?"

"Well, it did cross my mind."

"So what are you going to have?"

"I am going to either settle for the Mariner's Curry Shrimps, prawns, mussels, calamari and line fish in a mild curry sauce or the grilled or deep-fried Kingklip, but I think the curried option.

Why don't you have the Regatta Salad with smoked salmon, avocado and feta cheese?"

"Why not? That sounds like a good idea."

When our waiter returned we placed our order and

while we waited Helen continued to enjoy the view and relaxed setting.

Sitting outside waiting for our meal to arrive, Helen admired the long sandy beach, framed by mountains, while hoping to catch a glimpse of the local Cape seals that make the harbour their home.

"Isn't it beautiful here?"

"Is that a question or statement" I asked.

"No it's not a question, but a fact. How nice and warm it is as well." Helen said.

Before I had time to reply, she said

"I have just seen some seals!"

I knew by the tone in her voice she thought they were cute.

"Helen you might think they are cute, but you don't want to get to close to them. They don't smell too great, believe me."

The seal watching was interrupted when our waiter arrived with our food.

Stanley Dorman, a local resident built this, the first harbour front restaurant. His family had been part of Hout Bay for over 100 years. He decided to revamp the original workshop which was used for repairing his fishing fleet.

It was Sunday, and I had decided long in advance that this would also be our day of rest, before the trip hotted up.

After the leisurely lunch and tipping our friendly waiter we walked back to our car. I handed Helen some money to give to the car guard, who I knew would be waiting.

"Here you go Helen, you can give him the money, but don't give it to him until you are about to leave."

The waiting car guard was duly paid, and we travelled along Chapmans Peak, described as one of the most dramatic marine routes in the world, as it hugs the coast of the Atlantic Seaboard for nine kilometers.

This 9 kilometer toll road includes over 100 bends or curves as it follows the rocky coastline along some incredible views of the sandy bays below.

A number of rest areas are situated on this stretch of road where the motorist can stop and admire the views, take pictures or picnic.

Judging on once again the amount of "wows" from Helen, she must have found the views spectacular.

I had decided before leaving the UK, I would not chat too much while driving. I didn't want to distract Helen. She needed to give her full attention to the road and to the unbelievable amount of reckless and unlicensed motorists. In the UK drivers obeyed the rules of the road but this was South Africa, where people did what they wanted and didn't care about the outcome.

I would wait impatiently until we stopped the car before chatting or asking Helen what she thought. One thing I did know without even chatting in the car was she was really happy, and her happiness in turn made me feel good.

Next stop was Simons Town, a naval base. It took its

name from one of the Dutch governors Simon van der Stel.

During the centuries, the area has been under the control of the Dutch, the French, the British and finally South Africa.

After a visit to Simons Town, the next stop was Cape Point and the lighthouse.

Driving through Table Mountain National Park, a world heritage sight, Helen got to see her first baboon, which for some strange reason she seemed thrilled to have seen.

"Oh look there? I can't believe it!!!"

"You can't believe what" I asked.

"It's a baboon!!"

I doubt if many South Africans would feel the same way about these animals. Most would consider them to be pest; dangerous and at times vicious.

Arriving at the car park we bought our tickets and made our way to catch the Flying Dutchman as it is called. The Funicular runs from the car park up to slightly below the level of the old lighthouse. 100 steps later took us to a viewing platform at the base of the lighthouse.

While we stood at the top and I heard the sound of the crashing waves Helen said "it looks really wild out at sea. I would hate to see what it is like during a storm."

I don't know how, but on our way down, we managed to descend via a different route.

The Flying Dutchman takes visitors from the lower station at 127 meters above sea level, to the upper station at 286 meters above sea level.

This area was known as the Cape of Storms' by Bartolomeu Dias in 1488. At night and in fog, it was hazardous; with violent storms and dangerous rocks that over the centuries littered shipwrecks around the coastline.

The old lighthouse is no longer used and has been replaced with a newer building. In April 1911, the Portuguese liner Lusitania was wrecked just south of Cape Point, which prompted the relocation of the lighthouse.

The light of the new Cape Point lighthouse is the most powerful on the South African coast, with a range of 101km.

In the early years of the 20th century icebergs from Antarctica were occasionally sighted from Cape Point. No ice has been seen recently, which experts believe is due to global warming.

Our day of rest was almost over, and we decided to make our way back the 60 kilometers to Camps bay, via the famous Boulders beach, a favourite place for penguins.

Wooden walkways allowed visitors to view the African penguin colony without disturbing them. You could also swim if you wanted at Boulders beach.

When we parked the car Helen couldn't help noticing a sign which I bet you will not find any where else in the world.

It read 'beware of sleeping penguins under your car.'

"Look at all those penguins! They seem to be every where"

"Well Helen that's why we are here, for you to see the penguins" I replied.

So far so good!! Helen seemed to be enjoying South Africa. Perhaps it was the walk on the beach and trying to avoid the penguins, which seemed to be every where, or was it my expertise as a guide?

On our way back, it began to drizzle. We decided to pop into the V&A waterfront. This would be a quick visit. The major retail chains at this tourist attraction stayed open until late on a Sunday night, and we needed to get some snacks to take back to the guest house with us.

When we got back to the guest house Helen wanted to know how I could call black men "bubba", and black women either "mamma" or "ma". Wasn't this insulting?

I assured her it was not insulting, but those terms were friendly terms. "If you listen, some times they call me bubba as well."

"But you don't even know them" she persisted.

"Yes Penguin, you don't have to know someone to use those words. Remember, we are in South Africa now, and we are all friendly people."

The following day we were off to Stellenbosch, Paarl and Worcester.

Day 3

I know I described the previous day, a day of rest, which it was. We had only travelled 120 kilometres, but at least Helen got to see part of the fairest Cape, and wouldn't have to rely on pictures taken by other people, who she did not know.

While the scores of vineyards in Stellenbosch offer a selection of tasting options from biltong and wine, chocolate and wine, a bicycle tour and wine and private wine tours, we did not stop at any of the estates, but made our way to Koffieklets, one of the oldest buildings in the town.

The town is about 50 kilometers east of Cape Town, along the banks of the Eerste River. It is the second oldest European settlement in the province, after Cape Town. It became known as the city of oaks, after its founder Simon van der Stelplanted many of these trees.

Just like Worcester and a few other towns, Stellenbosch has a system of furrows alongside the roads, which carry irrigation water for the adjacent plots.

Once again yogurt for breakfast and biltong for Marko and then Koffieklets, here we come!! I wondered what traditional cakes would be on the menu.

We found parking under the shade of one of the numerous oak trees and made our way to the coffee shop, one of the oldest buildings in the town.

This would be Helen's chance to savour koeksisters, milktert and drink some "boeretroos" coffee.

The koeksisters were an instant hit, and fortunately for her, the shop sold freshly baked packets of this traditional pastry.

On our way out Helen said "I'm so glad we stopped here, and I really love those koeksisters."

"I said you would like them didn't I?"

With 2 packets of koeksisters in the car, we drove to Butterfly World near Paarl and spent a couple of hours looking at all the specimens.

Once again Helen was taken aback at the vast array of colours compared to the butterflies found in the UK.

From Paarl we made our way to Worcester, mainly to show Helen where I went to school.

By the time we got there in mid afternoon, it was already 35°c, and unfortunately the school was closed, but one of the administration staff gave us a brief tour of the premises.

On our way to Worcester we drove through the 4 kilometre Huguenot Tunnel in the Du toitskloof Pass Mountains, but on our way back to Camps Bay we decided to drive the original and more scenic route over the mountains.

It is hard to believe that this 48 kilometre stretch of road over the mountain was built by about 500 Italian prisoners of war under the direction of the National Roads Council.

Driving through the wine lands of the Cape, Helen noticed with alarm and despair her first sighting of an open ended pickup truck known as (bakkie) carrying black people on the back of it. These would invariably be driven by a white driver.

This would be the first of many as we made our way around the country.

"Look at that? That is so dangerous. How can they allow it?" She asked with an incredulous tone in her voice.

"What is so dangerous?" I asked.

"I have just seen a bakkie as you call them with about 15 black people on the back of it, and most of them standing."

"They don't allow it, but people do it, and I can tell you, that won't be the only bakkie you see carrying people" I informed Helen.

110 Kilometres later we were back in Cape Town, and on our way to Camps Bay and to the pool for a swim, say hello to Marko, and to get ready later that evening to visit Gold restaurant.

The restaurant claims to offer the visitor a dining experience with a selection of dishes from across the African continent, with each dish followed by African drumming and dance.

Before tucking into your meal you are offered a welcome drink, where you are taught ways to play the drum and to make two distinctive sounds with it.

The evening ends with all the waiters and kitchen staff

gathering in the dining section to sing and dance.

For me, I thought the food on offer was not very good, and I doubt how authentic some of the dishes were.

However, for tourists I guess the food was not the main menu but more so the singing, dancing and the drumming.

Judging on the amount of laughter, I know Helen enjoyed her self.

Day 4

After sharing a leisurely breakfast with Marko we dressed and made our way to the V&A waterfront.

The Waterfront is a working harbor, and offers over 250 shops from designer boutiques to craft stalls, a host of restaurants and coffee shops and plenty of activities for children. The Two Oceans Aquarium, the Telkom Exploratorium, and The SA Maritime Museum with its interactive displays, featuring history of local shipwrecks and more and the new Nelson Mandela Gateway in the Clock Tower exhibiting historical and educational material relating to Robben Island.

The area on the docks is made up of 2 large shopping centers, and next to them, the Red Shed Craft Market filled with a mix of traditional handmade items and art, and the world famous two oceans aquarium is also near by.

You can also sit outside at one of the many restaurants and watch the seals at play.

Boat trips are available to in and around the harbour and up and down the coast as well as to Robben Island from one of the quays.

We first visited various stores, which allowed Helen to see what was exclusively available in South Africa, before making our way to the two oceans for a tour of the aquarium.

Having looked at the various inhabitants swimming in all the tanks, we went out to one of the quayside restaurants for lunch.

There were several restaurants to choose from, and we decided to try a Portuguese restaurant.

I was looking forward to a prego roll, but was disappointed. Helen had the same, but as it was her first prego, she wouldn't have known if it was good or not.

While the food was average, Helen did enjoy the view of the waterfront. After lunch we took a walk down to where the boat trips departed from, with offers of 1, 2, 3 hour and sunset cruises.

"Penguin, shall we go on a boat cruise?" I asked.

"That sounds like a really good idea" she said.

By this time it was mid afternoon, so we chose to do a 2 hour trip around the harbour.

The skipper-guide was very good pointing out all the sights, and stopping to allow his passengers to take as many pictures as they wanted.

"Look!! There's a seal. Look there's another one, and wow, another one" said Helen.

Returning to the quay, we made our way back to the guest house and to spend our last night with Marko.

It would be an early night as Helen had a journey of over 400 kilometres the next day, and this would be her first long journey in South Africa.

Before leaving the next day, we had to visit Canal Walk one of the largest and most modern shopping malls with its 400 shops in the country to have her suitcase either repaired or replaced.

Where to get a quick bite to eat I wondered? Bonnie and Clide suggested the Ocean basket, a takeaway at the bottom of our street.

Ocean Basket opened in 1995, and now has numerous branches through out the country, and is the leading retailer of its sort.

This fast food outlet was not on the "places to eat list, but what the hell, it was near by.

They said we could walk, but as it was getting late, we decided to drive there.

Once again, a car guard was there to show us where to park.

When we got out the car, we also noticed there was a KFC near by.

"What is it to be?" I asked Helen.

"How do you mean?"

"Do you want chicken or fish?"

"I don't mind"

"I think fish. You haven't tried Ocean Basket."

We ordered fish and chips, something simple, and took our catch back to the guest house.

Day 5

As I previously said, I have an abiding interest in shopping malls. Quite why I do, I really do not know, but perhaps the only explanation I have, is I like to find out what speciality shops each mall offers. Forget about the local and international chains.

Canal walk also features a unique Afri-Bizarre, which promotes the work of local retailers and craftsmen.

Play facilities for kids are also not forgotten. With descriptive names such as the Magnetic Climbing Wall, Lazermaze, Slippery Slide and Three-Storey Jungle Gym. Place of Play as it is called puts a big emphasis on safety, with each child given a wristband to ensure that they can't leave the premises without being noticed.

For movie fans there are 17 cinemas to choose from, as well as a massive gaming hall for older kids.

On its doorstep, you will also find other attractions like Intaka Island, the award winning wetlands and eco-tourism attraction spanning 16 hectares; Ratanga Junction, South Africa's first full scale theme park, with over 30 rides; Golf Village, with driving range and all the necessary facilities for refining your game.

Enough enough I hear you say about this shopping mall, and I agree, especially seeing I am not been paid to promote them.

However, before I and we move on, I must tell you that the broken in suitcase was replaced, and Helen got to have a corn dog, not available in the UK but standard fair in the US.

Another surprise was waiting for her when we went to fill up with petrol.

She couldn't believe that at every petrol station there was a friendly attendant to not only operate the pump, but also clean the windscreen, check oil and water and if need be even check tire pressure, and all that without even having to get out of the car.

"How great is that. I don't even have to get out of the car. I think I am getting to like your country even more" she said.

It was etiquette and expected of the motorist to pay the attendant a tip each time he or she filled up at a petrol station.

With a full tank, and the brand new suitcase safely in the boot, we set off for Mossel Bay along the N2.

This highway begins outside the entrance to the Victoria & Alfred Waterfront, and takes one past Somerset West, then over Sir Lowery's Pass to enter the Overberg region. It passes near the town of Grabouw on the Hottentots-Holland plateau before descending the Houwhoek Pass to Botrivier. After Botrivier it makes its way across the agricultural plains through the towns of Caledon, Riviersonderend, Swellendam and Riversdale to once again hug the coast at Mossel Bay, which marks the beginning of the Garden Route.

We stopped at Swellendam, about half way between Cape Town and Mossel Bay.

The town is Over 250 years old, with wide streets, neatly preserved Cape Dutch and Victorian buildings.

After the refreshment break and a brief chat, it was back in the car again and next stop Mossel Bay.

This coastal town has always been associated with early European explorers.

Bartholomew Dias sailed into the Bay in 1488 unaware that he had in fact rounded the Cape of Good Hope and 9 years later, Vasco Da Gama also visited the area calling it Aguada de Sao Bras (the watering place of St. Blaize). While there, he negotiated for cattle with the local Khoi in what is generally regarded as the first commercial transaction between Europeans and the indigenous peoples of South Africa.

3 years later Pedro d'Ataidetook shelter in Mossel Bay after most of his fleet was destroyed by a storm. The sailor left a note of his journey and the disaster hanging from a Milkwood tree in a shoe.

Miraculously, the report was discovered one year later, and since then the tree has served as a kind of a postal clearing house.

The tree is a national monument and is generally known as the Post Office Tree.

The post box at the Old Post Office Tree can be used to post postcards and letters. A special frank is used on all outgoing mail to commemorate the fact that South

Africa's first post office was this tree! The reason for the boot-shaped letter box is that it is presumed that the first letters were left at this old tree from the 1500's in a sailor's boot!

My last visit to Mossel Bay had been several years earlier, when SAA took all the local aviation journalists for a weekend break to this Southern Cape town.

When we got to Mossel Bay we made our way to the beach and a restaurant and sat outside enjoying the sound of the surf and sight of the sea.

"Penguin, how are you feeling after your long drive?" I asked.

"I'm fine, but really don't like the highways. There is not much to see, and you always have to be alert in case any of the idiots makes a mistake. I saw so many drivers take chances.

It looks to me if every one is in such a hurry and most of the drivers have no consideration for other people on the road."

"I agree, but what do you expect when probably more than half the drivers have got their licenses fraudulently and the other half probably shouldn't even have their cars on the road?" I said.

"It certainly looks like it."

"Helen, just remember, when ever you want to stop for a rest, just say so. There is no hurry. It doesn't matter what time we reach our next destination."

"Yes I know, but I also want to get there, and chill out once there." She said.

"Anyway, what do you fancy for lunch?"

After studying the menu, Helen said "I think I will try one of their steaks."

"Which one" I asked.

A pause followed before she said "How about the fillet steak with green peppercorn sauce?"

"Well, if that's what you want then order it. I am going to have fish." I said.

After lunch, we drove on to the post office tree and wondered around the area for a while.

Our journey for the day was not over; we had to get to Oudtshocrn some 90 kilometres away over the Robinson pass.

We arrive shortly before 6pm at Die Fonteine guest house, and were greeted and welcomed byAnzue and Pierre, the owners, who introduced us to their two dogs, a jack rustle and a collie.

Once we had been shown to our room, and unpacked we joined the owners on the veranda for some home made ginger beer and when they heard about Helen's love for koeksisters, 3 suddenly appeared on a plate for her.

As we sat chatting on the veranda drinking ginger beer, and Helen enjoying her koeksisters, the dogs decided to join us.

We had both forgotten that this guest house did not have a swimming pool, but fortunately for us with the temperature that day peaking at 40°c, our room did have air conditioning.

While I continued chatting to the owners, Helen went and had a relaxing bath.

Her time in the bath might have been relaxing, but when she got out of the bath, she noticed a stream of water slowly making its way across the bathroom and bedroom floors.

Helen, a natural worrier, first thought she had been the cause of the miner flood, but after calling Pierre, who quickly discovered where the leak had come from began mopping up the floors while at the same time apologizing for the inconvenience.

Leak now plugged, and floor dry, we gave the 2 dogs some biltong, and we went to bed.

After the long drive, an early night was most welcome.

Day 6

ext morning, we once again woke up to the call of the Hadeda, and when we opened the door, found 2 dogs waiting on the mat outside the door for us. Against the owners instructions we let them into the room. They had told us, that if we let them in, we would never get them out again.

The best way to tempt a dog to move is to offer it some biltong, and it worked once again when we made our way to have breakfast with the dogs following closely behind us.

The breakfast was a typical Afrikaans meal. Fresh fruit, Eggs, bacon, sausages, and boerewors, all from the farm next door, along with freshly baked bread, and don't forget the boeretroos.

Oudtshoorn is best known for previously being the ostrich feather capital Of the world. Some 100 years ago many farmers became incredibly rich and were known as ostrich barons.

Today there are still many ostrich farms in the area, but it is no longer feathers that are in demand, but the meat, and many different ostrich leather products.

Ostrich meat in various forms is sold in many places, but never so more than in Oudtshoorn.

Ostrich steaks are now common place, but neck

of ostrich stew is also becoming a favourite. Sausage, salami, biltong and ostrich eggs, are just some of the other ostrich products and don't forget ostrich treats and bones for dogs.

Depending on your weight, you can also ride an ostrich.

Driving to the guest house the day before we had seen many ostriches in pens along the road.

Now away from Cape Town, Helen was beginning to discover true Afrikaner hospitality, not to mention food. The owners of Die Fonteine were a great example of Afrikaner hospitality and warmth.

Next on the to do list were the Kango caves, but before we got there, I would have to find a butcher and replenish my dwindling stock of biltong.

Biltong from supermarkets or specialty stores is fine, especially if there is nothing else available, but biltong from a butcher and better still, if he is Afrikaans can not be beaten for taste.

While driving to the Caves Helen said "I know I haven't been here very long, but I really do think the Afrikaners are so much more friendly than most of the English people we have met"

"Penguin, I agree with you, but wasn't going to tell you my thoughts. I wanted you to find out for your self."

The Cango caves are about 20 million years old and extend about 4 kilometres in to the mountain.

The main chamber in the Cango Caves is called Cango 1; containing countless dripstone formations, named

Van Zyl's hall after its discoverer, and is so huge that classical concerts were once held there. However, this was stopped after people began vandalizing some of the chambers.

Karen our guide told us that Cango one; is over 90 metres long, 50 metres wide at its widest point, and between 14 and 18 metres high. Nearly 100 metres of solid limestone roof separates the cavern from the outside.

Tourists are strictly forbidden to touch any of the formations.

However, when Karen noticed I was blind, she called for a pair of gloves. Wearing these gloves meant I was able to feel many of the formations.

To demonstrate the acoustics in Cango 1 Karen began to sing.

I could not believe what a melodious voice our guide had.

"Karen you should be on the X Factor. You would win with a voice like that" I said.

Karen just laughed. "Yes I enjoy singing, but don't think the X Factor is for me. I love my job too much."

The first thing I noticed entering the caves was how humid and warm it became. There was also a slight smell about it, but I couldn't say what it was, but I guess caves must have a certain smell about them even though I am not an expert in caves.

One of the highlights is Cleopatra's Needle: standing 9 metres high and is at least 150 000 years old.

Another highlight for me was being able to touch and tap the so-called drum; a naturally hollowed out formation, no doubt hundreds of thousands of years old and in the making, and it did sound exactly like a drum being beaten.

Some of the other stalagmites, stalactites and helictites resemble the beak of a Giant Eagle feeding its chick, the Outstretched Lost Wing of an Angel, and the so-called Bridal Chamber with its fourteen post bridal bed.

One hour later we were back out in the fresh air and under the hot sun.

This was my first visit to the caves, and I know Helen found it just as interesting and spectacular.

Next on the list that day was the Cango WildLife ranch with its various big cats, reptiles and other animals.

After paying the entrance fee, we joined a guided tour to take us around the site.

The wooden walkways allow the visitor to look in to the enclosures where the animals are kept.

The animals we saw that day included: white lions; cheetah; Bengal tiger; serval; lemurs; Common marmoset monkeys; African bush pig; bat-eared fox; blue duiker; Cameroon dwarf goat; Cape porcupine; Malaysian flying fox; pygmy hippopotamus; slender-tailed meerkat; Asian water dragon; crocodiles; lizards and monitors including collared iguana; inland bearded dragon and giant day geckos.

Snakes included: African puff adder; boomslang;

black forest cobra; black mamba; boa constrictor; albino Burmese python; Cape cobra; East African green mamba as well as tortoises and turtles and finally some birds like the Cape vulture.

Admittedly, the vast collection of animals we saw were not free roaming, nor were many South African, but at least Helen had seen them in real life, and not just on the TV.

After walking through the ranch, Helen returned to the cheetahs. She had booked to do a one-on-one encounter with a couple of cheetah cubs. She sat in the enclosure and stroked them, while the guide stood near by and watched.

"I was at first a bit nervous, but it was great. I never thought I would ever get the chance to stroke a cheetah" she said.

When we left the ranch I wondered if the Pygmy Hippopotamus like its much bigger and heavier brother which can weigh up to 4 tons attacked and killed as many people in Africa. I thought, may be it only killed little people or Pygmies, but I will never know.

One animal which did kill people both little and large was the Nile Crocodile and we and the other people on the tour got to see this creature leap some 2 metres out of the water to snatch a lump of meat held in mid air by the guide.

After a quick bite to eat at the restaurant; we made our way to the Swartberg Pass, which runs between

Oudtshoorn and Prince Albert.

The pass is one of the steepest in the country, climbing 1000 metres over a 27 kilometre stretch of gravel road between the 2 towns. It is also a national monument and a world heritage site.

Thomas Bain, who was responsible for many present passes began work over 100 years ago on this his last site.

He used over 200 convicts to build the 27 kilometre road over the mountain.

The convicts used: Pickaxes, spades, sledgehammers, crowbars, wheelbarrows and gunpowder were used during the construction. Boulders were split by heating them with fire and then throwing cold water over them. Rocks were then broken into smaller pieces with sledgehammers. The dry-wall method of construction was used to build the impressive retaining walls that supported the road against the steep slopes. Even 130 years later, travellers still wonder how he managed to do it.

The dry stone packed retaining walls are amazing; in one place the wall is 2,4kms long. They range in height from ½ metre to 13 metres.

The ruins and remains of the convict stations can still be seen in the Swartberg Pass.

Driving slowly up and over the gravel road pass, and carefully negotiating the numerous hairpin bends, Helen stopped several times to take pictures of the striking warped and twisted rock formations and the different plants.

Starting our drive up the pass, it was about 38°c, and by the time we got to the top and got out of the car, the temperature had dropped to 15°c. After the constant heat of the past few days, it felt quite chilly.

"I can't believe how cold it is up here" she said.

"I know, you wouldn't believe about 30 minutes ago we were both so hot"

When we reached the bottom and after a short drive to Prince Albert, we stopped at one of the nicest tea rooms we had yet found.

Sitting outside we enjoyed a cup of tea and iced coffee and the best milktert to date.

"I do really like it here."

"But Penguin, you haven't seen much if anything at all of the place." I said.

"I know, but there is just something about this place. I can't tell you what, but I know I want to come back here again."

"Penguin, how can you be so sure?" I asked.

"Don't ask me, but I know I want to come back here."

When we went to pay, the tea room owner told us about a particular place at the river where we could stop and swim.

On hearing this news, we left in a hurry to find this magic place, and to cool down.

The road we took back to Oudtshoorn via Meiringspoort and de rust meant we had to cross the same river 32 times.

We finally found the place, and after climbing up a pathway and over boulders, we came to the spot.

Once there, Helen changed in to her swimming costume, and clambering over a few rocks went in to the crystal clear water.

"Come on, get in and join me" Helen asked.

"No thank you, I am quite happy to sit on this rock and relax" I said.

We had the river and the pool to our selves for the next 60 minutes, until it was time to leave and get back to the guest house.

Arriving back, home made ginger beer was waiting for us on the veranda.

It also didn't take long for the dogs to find us, as they came to us with tails wagging.

I would like to think it was to see us, but most likely the anticipation of biltong might have lead their noses to us.

After a chat and shower, we made our way into town and to a restaurant for a meal. Let me hasten to add, I did have ostrich.

Helen wanted something Italian, while I was going to have ostrich in one form or other.

We went to Bello Cibo, and it didn't take us long to decide.

"I'm going to have the Tagliatelli Salmone Affumicato
"What is that?" I asked.

"Well according to the menu it is pan-fried smoked

salmon, with peppers and onions in a cream sauce, served with fresh lemon wedges.

I think you should have Tagliatelli Di Struzzo."

"I might, if you tell me more about it."

"It says it is pan-fried ostrich fillet with crispy bacon, mixed mushrooms and courgettes in amarula cream sauce."

"That sounds good enough for me. Are you going to at least try a little bit of mine?"

"I'll try a bit just to please you."

"You can't have come all the way here, the ostrich capital of the world, and not even tried a bit of ostrich."

As we waited for our meal to arrive, we sat and spoke about the day. We had seen and done so much, even though it was almost 40°c.

"What did you enjoy the most?" I asked.

Helen sat for a moment and then said "I think first must be playing with the cheetah cubs, and then the swim in the river."

"For me, it was the Cango caves. I found them really interesting."

Day 7

The next morning once again after a leisurely breakfast and collecting some bottles of the home made ginger beer and a couple of packets of koeksisters which we had ordered, we left Oudtshoorn for Sedgefield via George.

The 85 kilometre drive would take us back to the coast and thankfully to slightly cooler weather.

The village of Sedgefield was originally a farm. Tourists across the country are attracted to it thanks to the mild weather through out the year, the unspoilt beaches, and many water activities. It is also close to Knysna.

The town's motto of being a place where 'the tortoise sets the pace', probably best describes this popular site.

A few of the highlights in the area include, the Saturday Wild Oats market with its wide variety of fresh produce and local crafts attract visitors each weekend.

Local natural attractions include Gericke's lookout point which resembles the profile of a resting lion, along with the protected natural dune areas with their Cape Fynbos plantations and rare birdlife.

If the countryside was not enough, there are also numerous rivers, 5 lakes, beaches, some stunning mountain ranges, and the largest stretch of historical indigenous forest south of the equator.

Our destination this time was an Eco Friendly Tree

house some 23 kilometres from the village and Set in indigenous forest and overlooking a gorge.

When we arrived, we met the owner Robbyn, who then hopped on her scooter and we followed her to the tree house.

The tree house comprised a tented bedroom and fully equipped kitchen and an outside shower.

"This looks really cool!" Helen said as she admired our next place of rest.

"But" I said "remember there might be some spiders".

"What do you mean?"

"Well, it is out in the open and in the forest, so there are bound to be some spiders somewhere."

At least this place had a swimming pool, even if it was a converted farm dam.

According to the brochure guests could sleep, eat and shower in the canopy of the forest, surrounded by bird song and butterflies.

However, what it failed to mention and Helen would find out later, it also included spiders.

Most people would simply find these creatures an inconvenience, but Helen has a fear of spiders no matter what size or shape. Her immediate reaction is to find any heavy object, and aim it in the direction of the unsuspecting arachnid.

After saying goodbye to Robbyn, we unpacked, and then made our way back to the swimming pool.

While Helen enjoyed the cool water, I went and

stretched out under the shade of a big tree.

It wasn't long before the owners 2 dogs, a lab and a collie joined me.

When Helen returned she found all 3 of us asleep under the tree.

Shortly after my nap, Robbyn appeared again, and took us down to show us her horses, with the dogs following us.

The evening was approaching, and it was time to drive to Knysna to visit the weekly Friday food market, with its numerous food stalls. Robbyn had assured us we would find something to eat from the selection of food stalls.

Yes, there was a variety of foods on offer, but nothing we really fancied, so we made our way to the town to see what we could find.

There are two problems when you are in a town and firstly you don't know where to go, and secondly, where to find a restaurant.

After driving around for about 20 minutes looking for some where to eat, we finally found a branch of Panarottis, the pizza and pasta restaurant.

"Do you want to try them? They are on our to do list of food places." I said.

"Well we might as well.

Panarottis opened its doors in 1989, and 10 years later was the first Italian restaurant to sell the family-size pizza measuring almost half a metre.

There are 49 outlets in South Africa, and at present 6 internationally.

We parked the car and went in and were shown to our table.

"What would you like to drink?"

"I think I am going to have a fruit juice." Helen said.

When the waiter arrived, I ordered a fresh orange juice for Helen and I had a coke.

"Right, let's have a look at the menu."

While I waited, Helen read through the menu and with a surprised tone in her voice said "You can tell we are in South Africa."

"Why's that?"

"Well they even have a biltong and boerewors pizza! I know you don't like pizza, but may be you should have that one. I see they also do Wheat and gluten-free bases. Which are also yeast, sugar and egg-free."

"I might like biltong and boerewors, but not on a pizza. That's a waste. I think I will probably have one of the pasta dishes.

What about the deserts? What do they have there?" A short pause followed before Helen said

"You will probably like one of these. Fudge Picasso Slice

A white chocolate mousse, loaded with chunks of home-made fudge, coated with a white chocolate ganache and painted with strokes of dark chocolate and served with cream or ice cream.

Or how about Mississippi Mud Pie

A rich chocolate brownie base blended with pecans

or walnuts - buried under a thick layer of decadent hazelnut and chocolate mousse, covered with ganache and sprinkled with roasted Californian almonds, or Black Forest Cake

Traditional German torte transformed into a mouth-watering individual dessert, layered with cherries, chocolate and fresh cream and topped with fine chocolate shavings also with cream or of ice cream.

Any way, back to the pasta dishes. You can have any type of pasta with these. Chicken Capriccio which is oven-roasted chicken, assorted peppers and sliced button mushrooms in a cream-based sauce, or Carne, crispy bacon, spicy Italian sausage, salami, onions and assorted peppers, sautéed and combined in a creamy tomato-based sauce, or Saltimbocca, Fillet medallions, sautéed in herbed olive oil, served on a bed of fettuccini layered with mozzarella cheese and finished with crispy bacon, ham and sliced mushrooms in a rich, cream-based sauce or, seeing that you like spinach and chillies how about this one? Chicken and Spinach Fettuccine

Tequila-flamed peppers, chillies and oven-roasted chicken in a creamy tomato and spinach sauce.

I know you don't like pizza, but you can have their Santa Fe, a Spicy Italian sausage, salami, mushrooms and pineapple or Club Deluxe which is Roast chicken, bacon and ham, smothered in sweet-chilli mayonnaise.

How about Meat Supreme, Bacon, ham, Italian sausage and Bolognaise mince, in a cheesy BBQ sauce.

Even better, how about Carnivore? This pizza has Salami, spicy Italian sausage, bacon and ham, and now for your favourite, Biltong and Boerie pizza boerewors marinated in sticky BBQ basting with biltong and avocado."

"I am going to have the Saltimbocca and the Black Forest cake, and if I still have some room left, may be a Dom pedro. What about you?"

"I don't know, what do you suggest?"

"I think you should have the Club Deluxe or the Meat Supreme."

"I don't know. You choose for me."

"Right, then it will be the Club Deluxe and for your desert the Fudge Picasso Slice."

As we waited for our meal to arrive, we chatted about the day, the drive to Sedgefield, the tree house and our plans for the following day.

After our meal, we drove back to the tree house. When we got back, the first thing Helen did was to check if any uninvited spiders had taken up residence in our absence.

Fortunately for any unsuspecting spider, none had visited the tree house while we were away.

The next day we were of to sail the waters of the Knysna lagoon.

Day 8

We awoke to the sound of the numerous bird calls including my favourite, the Hadeda.

While Helen went to enjoy her first outdoor shower, I sat drinking a cup of coffee while listening to the numerous bird calls.

Sitting in the tree on a branch above the shower, Helen saw the Knysna Lourie, a truly colourful bird, and one that is not that often seen.

This rather large bird has a long tail with an orange-red bill and a white line just under the eye, contrasting with its mainly green feathers. In flight, the Knysna Lourie has eye-catching crimson primary flight feathers.

Once we had finished our cups of coffee, and packing up ready to leave, Helen saw a small spider. The fortunate spider had luck on its side. It was time for us to leave and head for the famous Wild Oats market.

The market certainly lived up to its reputation. There were so many beautiful things all home and hand made to buy, but we had to remember our baggage limits.

We each grabbed a toasted sandwich and drove to Knysna and to the lagoon to take command of a boat for 3 hours. Helen was going to skipper the boat.

Knysna is home to the sea horse, the rare Pansy Shell, the brightly coloured and elusive Knysna Lourie as well as the seldom seen forest elephants.

A feature of the lagoon is the so-called heads. These are a pair of huge brightly coloured cliffs lying at the mouth of the lagoon.

The town is also known for its annual oyster festival.

The forest includes the protected and valuable gigantic yellowwood and stinkwood tree, as well as white elder, ironwood, Cape beech, Cape ash, white pear, forest elder, and cherry wood tree.

Years ago a helicopter crashed in the impenetrable forest, and was only discovered by accident 7 years later.

Arriving at the quay, we met the company agent, who gave us a brief run down of the boat, and said if we ran into any difficulty, to call them on our cell.

Well, all was going well until we hit a sand bank and the motor cut out.

"And now?" I asked Helen.

"I don't know"

As our boat gently rocked from side to side, I said to Helen "I think we had better try and start the engine again, or else we won't be going any where."

We both took it in turns to try and start the engine, but try as we may, nothing happened.

"I know Helen, they said we should call them if there is a problem. Why don't you give them a call?

Helen took out her cell phone and I waited, and waited and waited.

"Penguin, why don't you call them?"

"I can't."

"What do you mean you can't?"

"You don't want to know." She said.

"I do want to know."

"Don't get cross with me, but I have no charge on the battery."

"You must be joking!! Did you not charge it before we left?"

"No, I forgot."

"So what are we going to do now?"

"We'll just have to wait until another boat comes by, or they realize we are not back and send someone out to find us." She said.

"That's bloody great. I will probably get sunstroke at this rate."

As you can imagine, we were both not in the best frame of mind and there was very little talk, each sitting at either end of the boat as we waited with no fellow mariners in sight.

"Well instead of sitting here doing nothing and going no where, we might as well try rowing."

We tried, but all we managed to achieve was the boat going round and round in circles.

"Well, if we don't return in 3 hours, I guess they might send someone out to find us."

After about 30 minutes, a boat appeared. We shouted to the occupants, but either they didn't hear us, or didn't want to help and continued on their way.

About another 30 minutes later, another boat appeared, and this time after explaining to them what had happened and asking them if they could phone the company, which they kindly did, we waited for help to arrive.

Some 15 minutes later help arrived, and of course, he managed to start the motor straight away.

After that experience I don't think I will be sailing around the world with Helen. As she was the skipper, I hold her to blame.

Back on dry land, it was time to leave Knysna and make our way on the N2 about 50 kilometres to nature's valley.

We followed The Knysna forests as it stretched on either side of the N2, but the beauty was spoilt by the erection of squatter camps next to the road.

When I last visited the area some 10 years earlier, there had been no squatter camps; in fact, the same could be said for many towns and even villages in the country. The inner city squalor which had been allowed to fester and grow now spread ever further outwards.

Nature's Valley lies virtually in the heart of the Tsitsikamma forest, and has only one shop, no banks, no shopping malls and as yet no squatter camps.

The village at the end of a winding gravel road consists of about 50 houses.

People visit the area to go for scenic walks, and hiking in the area through rainforest, along cliffs and through dry river beds.

Canoeing down the river, swimming or fishing in the

lagoon are some of the other activities guests can enjoy.

It didn't take us long to realize, the internet did not tell all about this guest house. It looked run down, needed much work done on it, and, Pat the owner was not that friendly and interested in her guests.

Fortunately, the guest house dog, a retriever, saved the day. She unlike her owner was friendly, and even without biltong walked uninvited in to our room.

That late afternoon we went down to the beach for a while before it started raining and we had to return to the guest house.

The only other nice thing about this guest house apart from the dog, were guinea fowl which could be heard in some near by bushes, another sound which reminded me of Africa.

"Did you hear what I heard?" I asked Helen.

"No what did you hear?"

"Listen."

"Oh yes, what bird is that?"

"Guinea fowl."

It was soon time to get back in the car and drive the 29 kilometres to Plettenberg Bay to look for restaurants, and to check out our destinations the next morning.

The following evening a former newspaper colleague Sharon, who I hadn't seen for almost 10 years, would be visiting us.

Long before Jan van Riebeeck landed at the Cape, Portuguese explorers charted the bay in the 15th and

16th centuries, the first being Bartholomew Dias in 1487. Ninety years later Manuel da Perestrello aptly called it Bahia Formosa or the Beautiful Bay. The first European inhabitants were 100 Portuguese sailors marooned here for 9 months when the San Gonzales sank in the bay in 1630.

The survivors built two small boats which they used to link with a passing vessel. In 1763, the first European settlers in the Bay were farmers and hunters from the Western Cape. However, Plet as it is known, was inhabited thousands of years before any European settlers arrived by Middle Stone Age man and then later by ancestors of the Khoisan.

At the mouth of the Keurboom's River the Bay hosts one of the largest seagull breeding colonies along the South African coast. The river is named after the indigenous Keurboom tree.

We were back at the guest house before the sun went down that night. There were no street lights on the gravel road, and Helen was not too sure if she would find the place in the dark. But we did.

We sat outside enjoying the tranquillity and playing with the dog until it was time to go to bed.

Day 9

Breakfast the next morning was similar to the guest house, nothing special.

With breakfast behind us, it was now off to visit the elephant sanctuary, and walk hand in trunk with these wonderful animals.

Before leaving the UK, I had pre-booked a 90 minute tour of the sanctuary for Helen. The tour included walking hand in trunk, feeding the elephants, brushing them down and watching them complete various commands.

When we got to the sanctuary, Lloyd one of the trainers asked me if I would like to go along with Helen, and he would guide me, while another trainer went with Helen and her elephant.

While I had originally no intention of doing the tour, but included it in our itinerary as something for Helen to remember, I found the whole experience incredibly interesting, and unforgettable. Why would anybody want to harm these peaceful and caring animals?

In fact, one of my books is about Lloyd this particular elephant trainer and his journey to become a trainer. The book is called Elephant Dreams.

At the end of the tour we were invited to have a cup of coffee and the guides would tell us more about their elephants and answer any questions. After question time, they played us a film of our visit and interaction with the elephants Obviously this was made with the hope that we would buy the DVD, which of course we did.

Before leaving the sanctuary we popped in to the curio shop. It scld so many items each with an elephant printed or modelled on it. We bought a print made out of elephant dung with an elephant footprint outlined on it.

As we walked out Helen said "That was amazing!!!"

"I agree, and Lloyd was really good. I think it was the first time he had taken a blind person on a tour, but as I have said before, the blacks don't have any hang-ups like white people when it comes to disability."

We had hardly anytime to discuss the events of the past two hours. Next on our to-do list that day was Monkeyland Primate Sanctuary virtually next door to the elephants.

This is the world's first free roaming primate sanctuary. All the different monkeys are free to move about the forest.

We decided to go on the one hour monkey safari with a guide.

Before we walked in to the forest, the guide gave each of the visitors some cream to smear on our legs to stop the mosquitoes from biting. He also warned the group not to touch any of the monkeys, and to remember that any monkey had the right of way, and we would have to simply wait until they moved off the path. "Remember this is their piece of land, you are a guest."

He also said that while many people think of monkeys as cuddly creatures, they can also be extremely aggressive.

With in minutes of entering the forest, it became apparent why we all needed the mosquito cream. There were thousands attacking any bare flesh they could find especially if you stood still for even a minute, which we often had to do when a monkey refused to move off the path.

We were also told to wait if one of the recognized aggressive monkeys was too close to the path.

There were monkeys of every size from miniature to quite big, different colours and shapes.

"Here's a little one, he or she looks so cute" Helen said as one attached itself to the bottom of my white cane.

"You won't say that if it decides to bite you" I said.

Half way through our forest walk we had to walk single file across a rope suspension bridge.

Before beginning the walk across the bridge we were told to remain still if a monkey appeared on it, and wait until he or she had left the bridge.

As you can imagine, all of us on that trip wanted to get across the bridge as soon as possible while the coast was clear. No one wanted to be stuck on the bridge with a monkey.

The brief safari was good fun, and I am sure the mosquitoes also enjoyed them selves.

I wondered if the owners of the sanctuary had signed a secret pact with the mosquitoes. "We will bring you as much food as you want, as long as you leave us alone".

With elephants, monkeys and mosquitoes behind us, it was now time for our feathered friends.

Fortunately the bird sanctuary, the world's largest single span aviary was right next door.

The two hectare dome houses over 2 thousand birds. The enclosure includes a gorge filled with lush indigenous forest, a river and waterfall. Within it are some 100 species of African birds, and a few species on the endangered list.

The dome is able to imitate a thunder storm, with claps of thunder and short cloudbursts from the irrigation system in the dome high above the forest.

The sanctuary has seven dams and a floating bridge with seating where you can order light meals; a 200-seater amphitheatre and a breath-taking canopy walk.

Unlike the 2 previous sanctuaries, this did not offer guided tours. At the entrance you were able to buy a booklet listing most of the inhabitants.

Helen, who has never been a particular bird lover, was quite interested, but the feathered friends couldn't beat the elephants, the cheetahs and monkeys.

It had been an exciting and interesting morning, and it was now time for lunch. We had something to eat at the restaurant as we watched and listened to the birds fly from tree to tree.

"This has been such a great day."

"Why so Penguin?"

"Well, what with elephants, monkeys, and birds, who

could ask for anything more?"

"You've forgotten one thing."

"What have I forgotten?"

"You forgot about the mosquitoes."

"Oh no I haven't, I can feel all the bites on my legs already."

After lunch, we decided it was time to drive the 38 kilometres to Bloukrans Bridge, the site of the worlds highest bridge bungee. It also marks the border between the western and Eastern Cape, with the arch bridge 216 metres above the Bloukrans River.

When we arrived at the bridge we pulled off the road, and walked down to a viewing platform to watch any bungee jumpers.

Apart from aspiring bungee jumpers and their families, there really isn't that much to see at this bridge.

We left and made our way back to the guest house to wait for my friend to arrive.

About one hour later while we were sunning our selves and playing with the dog, Sharon arrived.

After introducing her to Helen we sat around chatting until it was time to visit the restaurant we had selected in Plet.

Back again to Plet, and to the restaurant above the beach, with views of the surf, watch the sun go down while enjoying our meal.

By this time, Helen had got to know her way around Nature's valley so there was no hurry to get back.

We spent the next 4 hours chatting. Helen listened and laughed at some of the stories Sharon told about our exploits at The Star.

There are those special people we are lucky to meet, who even if you have not seen them for years can immediately pick up from where you left off when you last saw them. Sharon is one of these special people.

The other memorable thing about that evening was how well Sharon and Helen got on.

When we returned to the guest house, there was no sitting around and chatting until the midnight hour. We had to be up for what the establishment called breakfast, and after packing and loading our cases into the car, we said our goodbyes and followed Sharon on the way to Port Elizabeth some 213 kilometres away. We had to get to the airport to catch a flight to Durban later that morning.

There had not been much time to talk that morning. While in the car I asked Helen if she had enjoyed her self the night before.

"Yes it was fun, and I really like Sharon. What a lovely person, and great friend you have there."

Day 10

When we arrived at the airport, we dropped off the hire car, and made our way in to the departure terminal.

Even though it was a small airport, it was clean and easy to get around.

The Kulula flight took about one hour 20 minutes.

Kulula is one of the low cost airlines trying to compete against the state run SAA. The cabin crew was incredibly friendly and unlike every other airline their pre-take-off and pre-landing announcements were light hearted and humorous.

I would suggest to all that if possible use this airline.

At about 2pm we landed at King Shaka, Durban's newest airport built for the soccer world cup.

As per usual, Durban was hot and humid.

After collecting our car, it was time for Helen too hit the high ways of Durban.

The city traffic would be completely different to what she had experienced in the past few days.

Our first stop en route to st Lucia would be Richards Bay about 180 kilometres away.

There were several reasons to stop at this town.

Firstly, we needed to fill up with petrol, and then we needed to get some tablets for upset stomachs, and finally find some food to take with us.

Our final destination that day Toad Tree lodge near Hluhluwe

Was still another 80 kilometres away, and it wouldn't be long before the sun went down.

Things were going well until we came across a split in the road, and of course, there was no sign post to tell us which way to the lodge in the nature reserve.

Yes you would be right!!

We took the wrong road. It was now dark, and we were travelling slowly down an extremely wet and narrow gravel road, looking for our guest house.

Slipping and sliding down the road and Helen becoming more anxious as the minutes went by, we eventually decided to turn round and make our way back to where the road split.

What made it worse; there was 2 metre impenetrable grass and bush on either side of the road, and not knowing where you were, you didn't know who or what might be waiting to ambush you.

When we were finally able to get a cell signal, we phoned the manager of the complex Johan, only to be told that we had taken the wrong split.

Back we went slipping and sliding until we reach the original split and with much relief, made our way in the dark down another gravel road towards the lodge.

Things would go from bad to worse, and Helen's headache also went from bad to worse.

When we arrived, the lodge had experienced a power cut. There was no electricity, it was almost 38°c, our food was cold and could not be heated up in the microwave and apart from the stars, there was no other light.

We waited in the car while Johan went to fetch a torch.

While at the lodge, Helen would have a close encounter with a spider and a giraffe.

Finally we got our suitcases inside. I had just sat down on the veranda, when I heard a loud shriek coming from the toilet area.

It was Helen, and not some wild animal. As she was about to sit down, she noticed a large spider in the top right hand corner of the cubical.

The idea of sitting down on the toilet while there was a spider near by let alone actually sharing the space with her was a definite no-no.

She rushed out and said "Where Is Your White Stick?"

"Why do you want my cane? I asked.

"Don't ask Why; Just tell me where it is."

My white cane has come in handy at various times, but this would be the first time it was used to dislodge a spider, which ran out, and was not seen again.

At about 2am in the morning, the electricity resumed, and the ceiling fan, the fridge and lights began working again.

Day 11

As the sun rose, Helen was able to view our surrounds. The lodge was set in the bush with trees and shrubs surrounded by long patches of grass. The deck and plunge pool overlooked the large bush lawn, but there was no time to swim this morning. There were also no zebra, warthog and wildebeest waiting to greet us.

During the night we had heard bush babies run and jump on the roof. We also woke up to see a friendly gecko on one of the walls.

We had to leave to get to St Lucia, about 30 minutes away for our hippo cruise.

St Lucia lies at the southern most entrance to the iSimangaliso Wetland Park, and was the first park in the country to be declared a World Heritage site.

It is home to five ecosystems: swamps; lake systems; coral reefs; beaches; wetlands; woodlands and coastal forests.

The Great St Lucia Wetland Park supports the country's largest population of hippos and crocodiles. It is also home to leatherback turtles, black rhino, leopards, over 530 species of birds, including greater and lesser flamingos, and some 36 species of amphibians.

Most people do not know, but the park supports more species of animal than the larger and more well-known Kruger National Park.

St Lucia is one of the few towns which ask visitors to be on the look out for hippos found sometimes wandering the streets. Monkeys and little duikers also find their way in to the surrounding streets.

We had booked a guided tour in a boat on St Lucia Lake, and if we were not there on time, it would throw the itinerary completely out, and we would have to wait another 4 hours to go on the next tour of the lake.

After a quick bite to eat and a cup of coffee at KFC, we made it to the boat.

We were joined on the boat by a group of twitchers. The middle-aged group seemed to be more interested in the common weaver, than the sight of hippos and crocs.

Before we landed back on Shaw, the skipper produced an up till then hidden away hippo tooth.

I couldn't believe the weight and size of it. No wonder it is one of Africa's most feared animals.

Following the rush to get to St Lucia that morning, once back on dry land, we spent the next hour getting to know the little town and to find a restaurant for lunch.

"Let's look and see if we can find some where that makes the famous Durban and Natal Bunny Chow." I said to Helen.

We tried about 3 restaurants, but either they did not sell them, or they had just sold out.

However, we struck it lucky with the fourth restaurant. They had Bunny Chow on the menu.

A Bunny Chow is half a loaf of bread with the middle

hollowed out and filled with the curry of your choice.

The Indian community in Durban sold this to those who wanted a quick curry takeaway.

Having told Helen all about this meal, unfortunately, their version was not that nice.

After lunch we made our way back to the lodge, and to relax and enjoy some time in the plunge pool.

At about 4pm we decided to go and look for one of the watering holes, hoping to see some of the animals in the reserve.

We found the watering hole, but no game.

We waited for about one hour but no animal appeared. I said to Helen "I think it is about time to get back before the sun went down."

We started our walk back to the lodge, and rounding a bend in one of the bush paths, not 5 metres away blocking our progress was a giraffe.

"Oh my God" Helen said in a hushed tone.

"What is it?" I asked.

"There's a giraffe"

"Where" I asked?

"It's just in front of us"

"Don't worry, why don't you walk up to him and say hello?"

"Don't be silly, this is no time to joke" she retorted.

To say Helen got a fright would be an understatement, but the giraffe seemed to be unperturbed and simply looked nonchalantly at us.

It was as if he was saying it was his reserve, his path, and he would move when he was ready to, not when we wanted him to move.

We had no alternative but to wait. There was no other pathway back to the lodge.

After about 10 minutes he decided he had enough of us humans, and turned and walked away. It was hard to believe that such a large animal could disappear in to the bush in such a short time.

A dip in the pool, some snacks and after a check for any uninvited spiders, it was time for bed, as we had an early start the next morning.

We wanted to be on the road by about 5am, as the journey of over 600 kilometres to Hazyview in Mpumalanga would take at least 7 hours, and I didn't want us getting there after dark.

Day 12

Hazyview is nestled on the slopes of the Drakensberg Mountain Range. Like Johannesburg, the town has a previous history of gold mining.

With its subtropical climate, the town is renowned for its bananas and mangoes. It is also close to the Kruger National Park, and most of Mpumalanga's private game reserves are found just east of Hazyview. The region is also used by (SAPI) the South African Paper Industry with millions of trees waiting to be logged.

The town gets its name from the haze that hangs over the area during the heat of summer.

We woke up to a steady drizzle, which certainly cooled things down, but with the cloud cover, visibility was not that good.

At this early hour, there were not that many heavily laden trucks on the road, but as the kilometers went by the traffic and the rain increased.

It was not only the trucks Helen had to deal with, but the N2 was in a terrible condition, with numerous pot holes and resurfacing taking place at regular intervals.

Each time we came to a strip of road earmarked for resurfacing, a woman holding a board would announce a 10 or 20 minute delay while you waited until traffic in the opposite direction had made its way past the resurface stretch of cordoned off road.

Once the last car was through, it would be your turn to travel down the one-way strip, and the process would start all over again.

Making our way slowly towards Hazyview, the rain got heavier, and with it the visibility got poorer. At times Helen could barely make out where the road was thanks to the amount of water on it and the spray from trucks and other vehicles.

A journey which would normally take about 6 to 7 hours took us almost 10 hours.

When we finally arrived at the guest house, and our suitcases safely inside, we spent time with Penny, the owner and her 2 miniature schnauzer dogs, one of the friendliest owners we had met on our trip.

While Helen chatted to Penny, I sat on the floor playing with the 2 dogs much to Helen's embarrassment.

"You can't sit on the floor and play with the dogs" Helen said.

"Why not? I am sure Penny doesn't mind"

After about 30 minutes, it was time to make our way down to the log cabin, and almost immediately, Helen fell in love with the place. Not only 2 lovely dogs, but a stunning air conditioned log cottage and if that was not enough, a spa on the raised wooden patio, and a Private barbecue area outside each cottage surrounded by indigenous bush. There was also a swimming pool near by.

I have to agree with Penny who says, "This ensures that Thulamela is much more than just another tourist destination.

Thulamela is An Intimate Place of Rest - a place where one can contemplate life, rejuvenate oneself and leave with a sense of tranquillity and peace of mind."

What she doesn't say however, is that her warmth and hospitality exceeds the exceptionality of the place.

That evening we both went for a dip in the spa, and after that bed called.

Day 13

The next morning and you guessed it; we awoke to the sound of the Hadeda and the Piet-My-Vrou and if that was not enough, we were treated to a wonderful array of fruit and a warm deli platter brought to our cottage.

Each morning we sat outside and while Helen marvelled at the view, I enjoyed the sounds of the numerous birds.

As we enjoyed our breakfast each morning, the 2 dogs would arrive, and of course they each received a handful of biltong.

"This is what I call a real guest house, and anything else after this will be hard to beat" Helen said as she finished her coffee and gave the dog another piece of my biltong.

"I don't want to leave here. I wish we could stay here for ever."

Even though there were many places to visit, it seemed wrong to rush things that morning.

Once we were ready to leave, we popped up to say good morning to Penny, and after chatting for a few minutes, left for the Panorama Route as it is called.

The panorama route with its natural wonders includes Bourke's Luck Potholes, the Three Rondawels, God's Window, the Blyde River Canyon and numerous waterfalls.

Bourke's Luck Potholes are cause by decades of churning

currents of water resulting in a series of cylindrical rock sculptures that look as though they belonged on another planet. The soil in the swirling waters presents a white, yellow and dark brown colour.

Next on the route are the Three Rondavels. These are three round mountain tops with slightly pointed tops, very similar to the traditional round or oval African homesteads made with local materials called rondavels. They were also once known as The chief and his three wives. The flat-topped peak represented Mapjaneng, famous for opposing invading Swazis, with the rondavels representing his three troublesome wives.

Another must see and must visit is God's Window. Once you have climbed up to the viewing point, you will be greeted by the Lowveld more than 900 metres below, as you look at the indigenous forests in the ravine, and waterfalls, with the striking cliffs plunging over 700 meters to the Lowveld and the Kruger National Park.

En route to the 3 sites, we stopped at a couple of waterfalls before making our way first to God's Window, but unfortunately, Helen could not see much as it was overcast.

From there we made our way to the pot holes. We clambered on to and walked across a series of metal bridges above them, and then on to some of the near by ridges so Helen could take some pictures.

All I remember about the pot holes was the incredible sound of the rushing water beneath us.

From there we drove to look at the Three Rondavels.

Later on, Helen said "let's go and look for a baobab tree."

About one hour later after driving through various African villages, we still had not found this baobab tree and decided to return.

On our return trip we once again stopped off at God's Window as the weather had cleared.

It was now about 1pm, and we decided to find a restaurant and have lunch.

The humidity of the Lowveld or Mpumalanga had returned as we sat outside enjoying another prego roll.

Ten minutes later, we drove past a pancake bar. Helen said "I know I have just had lunch, but we have to sample one of their pancakes.

Before we returned to the guest house, we stopped off at a local butcher to pick up some meat for a braai or barbecue that evening.

Helen wanted some lamb Sosaties - kebabs marinated in apricot and curry sauce which are uniquely South African, some steak, and I wanted some boerewors.

Back at the guest house, we first went for a swim and then made our way to see Penny, and spent a couple of hours chatting.

That evening, while Helen attended to the braai or barbecue, Penny's young son and daughter and the 2 dogs came to visit us.

After they left, sadly it would be our last time in the spa before bed time, and our journey was almost over.

Day 14

The day began as so many had done over the past 14 days with the sound of the Hadeda and Piet-My-Vrou and other birds, but soon these sounds would be just a memory.

We sat outside for the last time enjoying a cup of coffee, while waiting for our breakfast to arrive.

After breakfast and with heavy hearts we packed and went to say our goodbyes. Penny invited us to have a look round her house, and to have a cup of coffee before we left.

Johannesburg and Muldersdrift 350 kilometres away waited for us. We were on our way to the cradle of humankind.

The trip to Johannesburg was without incident; however, Helen did become a bit nervous as we got closer to the city she saw 2 signs warning motorist that highjackers and thieves operate in the area.

By mid afternoon we had made it without being high jacked or met any thieves.

The guest house was nothing special. Unfortunately our experience at Hazyview had set the bar high, and it would take a lot to beat it yet alone equal it.

After unpacking and meeting the receptionist, and the guest house dog, we decided to drive around the area to make sure we would find our way to Maropeng the next morning.

We had dinner at the guest house, and after watching the sun go down, went to bed.

Day 15

Maropeng and our last day.

The Cradle of Humankind is believed to be the birthplace of Homo sapiens, and is one of 8 world heritage sites in the country.

The fossils are trapped in a case of dolomite thousands of years old.

Some of our ancestors discovered at the cradle of humankind include the skull of a 2 million year old known as Mrs Ples, and Little Foot 3 million years old.

More recently, new fossils have been unearthed and put on display: a 2 million year old partial female skeleton and the fossil of a young boy. The first time that 2 hominid fossils have been found together.

Maropeng Visitor Centre is built in the shape of a burial mound, symbolic of the secrets of our ancestors buried deep underground.

The exhibits depict a journey of discovery from past to future and include such original themes as an underground boat ride featuring and interactive display of the earth and its history.

With in the area, there are 15 major fossil sites with the Sterkfontein Caves the best known.

After breakfast we packed our suitcases in the car for the last time and drove to the centre; it was not yet open apart from the curio shop. I found it quite amusing that the music coming out from the speakers happened to be songs by the Beatles. You would have thought that local African music would have been more appropriate.

When the centre opened, a guide showed us around, and after the tour, we went on the boat ride, which was pretty impressive.

With both of us on board the boat, we were taken on a 3 billion year old journey back in time.

The 150 metre trip through the interactive virtual cave begins with the ice age thanks to the help of Snow and ice making machines.

Next in our time machine or boat we arrived at what the world was like when it was completely submerged in water, and before that to the formation of the earth's crust and the shifting of the tectonic plates.

As we journeyed even further back in time we were greeted by a fiery ball of molten rock, and finally a black hole.

After disembarking from our time vessel Helen and I then had to walk through a 3 metre imaginary black hole, which I would place any amount of money on will be the closest we will ever come to a black hole.

Stepping outside and back in the present we each ordered and ate an ice-cream, enjoying the sunshine before leaving for the penultimate destination.

I had decided as a final stop-over Helen should experience the Carnivore restaurant, which offers a true

South African eating experience.

About 15 minutes later, after parking the car, we walked through a thatched walkway surrounded by indigenous gardens and a water feature.

Once in the restaurant, a huge open fire forms the centre piece surrounded by 52 Masaai tribal spears holding 15 different types of meat such as pork, lamb, beef, chicken, ribs, sausages as well as meats such as crocodile, zebra, giraffe, impala and ostrich.

When seated, a flag is brought to each table. Only when you have had enough and can't eat any more, the flag is lowered.

The meal starts with a traditional soup, and honey baked bread.

Fresh salads are brought to the table along with six servings of meat sauces to compliment the main meal.

Next to arrive is a hot cast iron pot placed in front of you, followed by two smaller cast iron pots containing pap and sauce.

When diners are ready, carvers bring the spears holding the meat from the fire, and begin to carve the cuts of your choice directly onto your plate.

At the end of the meat feast, and if you are still hungry, you can choose from five different desserts and a choice of coffees.

Believe it or not, but this palace of meat also caters for Herbivores.

It was now 4pm, and time to take our leave of South

Africa, and drive to the airport.

As we made our way towards the airport, a typical Johannesburg afternoon thunder storm was heading towards the city, but Helen would have to wait for another occasion to experience this.

Holding my hand as she always did on take off, she did see some flashes of lightning as we passed through part of the storm.

Reaching cruising speed, I asked, "so Penguin, what do you think of South Africa?"

"It's great" She replied.

"Would you like to come back again?"

"Yeah, it's great, but there is so much to see and so much I haven't seen yet."

Leaving South Africa, my thoughts turned to the future of the Cape. It was depressing to think what would happen to Cape Town and the Cape Province, if the ANC ever got its dirty hands on both municipal and provincial authorities again.

Under the Democratic alliance (DA) things work. This can hardly be said for the other 8 provinces and almost all of the ANC controlled municipalities, with their corruption, fraud, non-payment of various suppliers, neglected hospitals with lifts not working, broken medical equipment, broken traffic lights, the breakdown of sewage works and municipal billing and service delivery problems, while officials enriched themselves.

My thoughts went back to the late 80s when the ANC

called on its lackeys to make the country ungovernable.

It was doing the same again, with various ANC leaders calling on their thugs this time to de stabilise the Cape and make the Province ungovernable.

What would Mandela think of this once democratic organisation, which these days claims it supports democracy, yet continues to do everything it can to take total control, and tries to suppress any opposition or criticism of it.

While I found the future somewhat unsettling, I couldn't help thinking back to what I had experienced and had forgotten about.

Unlike the British and many white people in South Africa, who are reserved, black people were non-judgmental, and accepting of people with disabilities. They lacked that awkwardness when meeting or interacting with disabled people; they did not feel self-conscious.

For years and on many occasions I had been lead hand in hand by black men and women, who did not find this type of physical contact unnatural, not something British or white South Africans would ever do.

Many South African white people might have material wealth, but black people enjoyed spiritual wealth, something no amount of money could buy.

It was also sadly ironic how the bottom of the pile had much in common with those at the top of the pile. Criminals at the bottom and various criminals at the top.

Another common factor between the bottom and the top was both had no respect for the laws of the land or the courts. Could one expect anything else from its citizens when the head of the country faces over 700 charges of fraud, corruption, money laundering, and racketeering and at one stage rape allegations?

"Would you like something to drink?" One of the cabin crew asked as my thoughts were interrupted and I returned to the present.

As we flew high above Africa, I was already thinking about the next trip, and where we might go the next time, and how many other places Helen would love.

Journey 2

Cape Capers

Day 1

"Welcome to Cape Town. We hope you have enjoyed your flight with us, and we hope we see you again, the temperature outside is 32°c."

We were back flying over Table Mountain, and back in Cape Town and ready to meet and get to know some more 4-legged friends, guest house owners, and strangers, view more wild life and of course enjoy more good food.

Once again the itinerary was set down page by page, and the Accommodation already booked. Helen also wanted her own to do list and a food places list.

I decided to give SAA another chance, but this time we would fly business class, and this was also one of the last direct flights between London and Cape Town by the airline.

Having travelled business class with the airline in the past, I wanted to see how affirmative action had impacted on service standards in this section of the aircraft.

This was Helens first trip in business class, and after experiencing the exclusive lounge area at Heathrow, she couldn't wait to begin her trip.

"If this lounge is anything to go on, I think I could get used to travelling business class. Just look at all the food and other things on offer" she jokingly said.

"Penguin, don't get too used to it" I said, and this time I was not joking.

"Any way, the flatbed will be wasted on you"

"Why, what do you mean?" She asked.

"Well, I bet you will spend the whole night watching movies."

"May be" she laughed and said.

Things went much better this time, especially when you consider how expensive travelling in the front of any aircraft is, but you would expect things to be much better wouldn't you?

I managed to get a few hours sleep, but Helen was not able to get much shut eye even if business class offered flatbed seats.

As I predicted, Helen chose to watch movies most of the time.

During the flight, I spent a few hours chatting to the cabin crew.

Most of the crew were from Cape Town, and one

member April told me about a really good restaurant she and her family went to.

April assured me, it was not on the tourist map, and only frequented by locals, but it did the best Malay curry in Cape Town.

Leaving the aircraft, April gave me a big hug, as if we had known each other for years.

Walking into the terminal Helen said "I can't take you any where."

"What do you mean?"

"As soon as my head is turned, you are off chatting up the cabin crew."

"Well, you don't expect me to sit for 12 hours without talking to anyone while you watch movie after movie? It shows you how friendly us south Africans are. We are not reserved like your bunch."

"No, I was only joking. I wish we in the UK were that open with each other."

Going in to the terminal, we waited and then collected our bags, and this time both were in tact.

Next we collected the hire car, and then switched on the satnav and drove to Tiger Valley Mall before making our way to Fishoek.

This shopping mall was included on the list for 2 reasons. Firstly we had to deposit some money, and secondly I didn't know of any butchers in the area, so would have to rely on biltong from one of the speciality shops, and of course, as previously mentioned, any excuse to visit shopping malls.

Mission complete, we then drove to Fishhook to find the guest house.

"I'm glad that's out the way. At least you have your biltong" she said as we walked out and back to the car.

"Oh, don't forget the koeksisters we got as well."

Fish Hoek is a coastal town on the eastern end of the False Bay side of the Cape Peninsula about 30 kilometres from the city.

Fish Hoek or Vissers Baai or Visch Hoek can be found on some of the earliest maps of the Cape. The arrival of Dutch settlers in 1652 soon forced the indigenous population to leave the area.

Previously the beach was used on an informal basis for whaling and fishing, but in 1918 it was laid out as a township.

For years, Fish Hoek was a "dry" area. One of the conditions placed by the original owner, who gave the land for development, was that no alcohol could be sold in fish Hoek. These days alcohol is available in restaurants and bars but there are still no bottle stores in the town.

In the summer months, the tourist season, Shark spotters are often on duty, on the look out for the Great White shark. From June through to November, Seasonal visits from Southern Right or white Whales occur and the bay provides some of the finest viewing.

We eventually found the guest house, and were welcomed by Bret, one of the owners and late that afternoon we got to meet his wife Sharon.

The cottage included a bedroom, dining and kitchen area and a bathroom.

There was a pool, but this had to be shared with the family.

One of the main reasons for choosing this guest house was the owners agreed we could stay there in the beginning for 2 days, and for one day at the end of our visit to the country.

After taking our suitcases to the cottage we decided to go for a swim, where we met the 2 family dogs.

"Hey, look at these really cute dogs!" Helen said.

"Helen I thought you would have been more delighted to be back in the Cape, and not just to find 2 cute dogs."

"Yes of course I'm glad to be back, but these dogs look so cute."

First we met a rather boisterous lab, and later a rather timid little dog of no particular heritage, but he soon forgot his timidity once some biltong appeared.

Our 4-legged friends would appear at the entrance to the cottage every time we were there and the door was open.

They would often both lie on the dining room floor, no doubt waiting for a tidbit.

That first night we decided to visit one of the local supermarkets and collect some bits for breakfast the next morning before looking for a restaurant.

Opposite the supermarket was a Spur steak house.

"Well Helen here is another family type restaurant you can add to your list of food places to visit."

The Spur steak ranch first opened its doors in 1967 and presently has almost 250 outlets in South Africa and a further 28 internationally.

Burgers, steaks and ribs are the main attraction. However, the restaurant does do a limited range of pasta dishes, seafood, chicken and vegetarian.

It is a family restaurant and the one feature found in most branches is a special children's play area.

It was still reasonably early, and we were able to get a table.

"So what do you fancy? Remember Penguin, they are known for their burgers, steaks and ribs."

"What are you going to have to drink?"

"I am going to have a mineral water, and you will probably have a coke?"

"Yes how do you know?"

"How about I am extremely observant."

"When are you observant?"

"I don't think there is a single time when we are out that you don't have a coke."

Before we continued chatting, I said "We had better decide on what to have to eat."

After Helen told me what was on the menu, I said "I think you would like either the Hawaiian Burger with a grilled pineapple ring, or their Goodie Burger with cheese, a pineapple ring and creamy mushroom sauce. Don't forget they come with crispy onion rings and chips OR a baked potato and if you don't want the onion and chips you can have their Garden Salad OR two hot veg. But I don't know if you are going to have a single or double burger."

"What are you going to have?" Helen asked

"It will be either the 200g Spur Fillet or may be the Portuguese Steak topped with peri-peri sauce and a fried egg, but I don't fancy the egg. I might have their extra matured prime cut of rump.

If I have the steak I can have either the Monkey Gland sauce, or Texan-Chilli, Garlic, Durky, Sweet Chilli or Peri-Peri sauce with my steak.

Mind you, the 2 pork spare Ribs and 3 queen Prawns with peri-peri sauce or lemon sauce could be an option.

But, Ribs and Calamari also sound kind of appealing, especially the Calamari.

I am not sure if I am going to have their onion rings and chips or their veg, depending if they have creamed spinach and if I am lucky pumpkin fritters."

"So what is it to be?"

"Well its going to be the goodie burger for you, and I am going to have the prime cut of rump with monkey gland sauce.

I know there burgers will be fine, but I don't know or rather can't remember what their steaks are like. After all, this is a family styled restaurant.

We didn't have to wait long before we gave the waiter our order, and our food soon arrived.

"Now that we are sitting down, how does it feel to be back again?"

"I love it, and the weather is lovely and hot."

Day 2

When I woke up just before sunrise, I was quite surprised and overjoyed to hear the Hadeda, but there it was, my personal reminder that I was back in Africa.

Later while we sat outside enjoying the warm Cape air and a hot cup of coffee, Helen got out the to do list.

"Isn't it great to be back?" I asked.

At first there was no reply. Helen was watching the 2 "cute" dogs.

"Yes it is. I do love being here" she said, but I told you that last night."

"Yes Penguin, but I had to check in case you had changed your mind."

First on the to do list was the Well known Old Biscuit Mill, which has become very much part of the Cape Town must visit places.

On our previous trip to Cape Town, one of the many places we did not have time to visit was The Old biscuit Mill in Woodstock.

We had heard and read so much about this market, and as Helen and I love going to markets, it was now the time to see what the fuss was all about.

As soon as we parked the car, we were immediately greeted by a car guard.

We were certainly not disappointed at the market. There was so much local and organic food, including cheese, breads, meats, cakes and biscuits, honeys, wines other refreshments, in fact, food from around the world but all made locally.

If you didn't like food; and I can't imagine why not, there were also locally designed clothes; home made soaps and candles; and many other items for the home; not to mention many novelty products.

Having sampled various foods, we found some where to sit and have breakfast before leaving for the world famous Kirstenbosch gardens. This was next on our to do list for the day.

The gardens at the foot of Table Mountain were founded in 1913, and cover an area of 528 hectares with 36 hectares of cultivated garden. They feature only indigenous South African plants. Fynbos, Proteas, cycads and rolling lawns blend together with streams and ponds and well-laid out pathways for easy walking.

In 1660, Jan van Riebeek ordered that a hedge of Wild Almond and brambles be planted to give some protection to the perimeter of the Dutch colony.

Sections of this hedge, named Van Riebeek's Hedge, still exist in Kirstenbosch. The hedge is a Provincial Heritage Site. The gardens in those days were used for the harvesting of timber.

Visitors now would find it hard to believe that just over 100 years ago, the gardens were overgrown, populated by wild pigs, overrun with weeds and planted with orchards.

The gardens now include many picnic sites as well as a restaurant, self-service area and tearoom, gift shops and a nursery.

On Sundays, during the summer months from November to April, musical sunset concerts are held on the lawns.

With time a factor, we chose to go on a one hour motorized tour. The guide stopped every now and again to explain about the various plants and how many were used in modern day medicines.

After the tour, we walked around some of the garden, before making our way to the gift shop.

Walking out of the shop Helen said "It is so lovely here. I wish we could be here when they have one of their evening concerts. It's such a pity we always seem to be in a rush."

"Yes, I know, but I want you to see as much as possible. Remember Penguin, we can always come back again the next time."

"What do you mean the next time?"

"Well, I imagine you would like to come back again next year wouldn't you?"

"I don't know. I'll tell you at the end of this holiday, and that's if we haven't come to blows before then." She laughed.

The gift shop was extremely disappointing. I don't

know why, but I was expecting it to stock many items from the gardens, but there was hardly any, and instead it was full of items which had nothing to do with the plants or the gardens.

Following Kirstenbosch, we returned to the cottage and the dogs, which appeared almost as soon as we unlocked the front door.

"Come inside doggies" Helen said as she unlocked the front door.

In the afternoon we went for a swim before getting ready to eat at the restaurant recommended by April, one of the cabin crew.

This restaurant was not on the tourist map, and more importantly it served genuine Malay Kerrie or curry dishes.

Helen was most put off to find that the mutton and chicken dishes came with the meat on the bone. This was never the case in the UK she assured me.

"How can they serve it with the bone still in it?"

"Why not, it adds to the flavour" I said, as I continued to enjoy and savour every mouthful.

Bone or not, it was delicious, and I would have returned the next day given half a chance.

Licking lips and fingers time over, we made our way to the Theatre on the bay.

"Shall we go back there tomorrow night?" I asked.

"I don't think so, and if you want to go back, you will have to find me a takeaway", a not too happy Helen replied.

We both love theatre, and I promised her that on this trip we would definitely take in a couple of shows.

Theatre on the Bay featured a musical comedy with a local cast.

Helen enjoyed the performance, but we were both surprised to find there was no programme for sale.

Enquiring why there was no programme, I was told the main reason for this was because the runs were so short. I must admit I found this a feeble excuse.

We went outside and paid the car guard for looking after our car and then drove the 32 kilometres back to the cottage.

In the morning, we would be leaving for Clanwilliam.

Day 3

An early cup of coffee, and a quick check on the to do list, before heading for a feast on the beach. After that it would be on to Clanwilliam, a total distance of about 260 kilometres.

Like our previous visit, I did not do much talking while on the highways. I wanted Helen to focus on the road, and more importantly keep a watchful eye on any reckless drivers.

We had to make sure we left reasonably early. The beach braai started at about mid day, and those attending were asked not to be late.

During our previous visit to the Cape, Helen had not explored or seen anything of the west coast, so this would be all new to her.

The road was fine until we reached 11 kilometres of road works, which slowed our journey down considerably.

It didn't take long to notice how drier this part of the Cape was, but the mountain scenery did make up for the bleakness.

The final stretch of the road to Muisboskerm where the beach braai was held was once again gravel.

"Oh no" Helen said.

"What's wrong now?" I asked.

"You'll soon find out".

Minutes later we began our journey on a gravel road, and I realized what she was talking about.

We arrived about 15 minutes late, but were still in time to enjoy the food and the setting.

Wind breaks made from branches surrounded the food and dining areas, and not far from it, the beach.

Walking in Helen said "this is amazing. The setting is really great. On the beach is the buffet, and behind it not far away the sea. They should really do something like this in the UK." She said.

The help your self tables included: Angel fish; Snoek; Yellow tail; a fish called hardies; Cape Salmon; mussels; fish curry, fish and rice and lobster.

If the selection of fish was not enough, there was also: mutton and lamb bredie; potatoe salad; sweet potatoe; freshly baked bread; homemade butter as well as homemade grape and fig jam; water melon, koeksisters and coffee.

Almost all the fish were caught that morning.

It was a case of eat as much as or what you want.

The setting and the food was great, and we both enjoyed our selves. It was also interesting to note, that we were the only English speaking people there. All the other diners were Afrikaans.

About 3 hours later we made our way towards Clanwilliam and to yet another wonderful guest house.

"That was really something different. I am glad you heard about this place. I bet not many English people know about it."

Nestled at the foot of the Cederberg Mountains, Clanwilliam is Rooibos!! The town is the centre of the Rooibos tea industry in the Cederberg, while factory visits and rooibos tasting is a must.

This is also one of the ten oldest towns in South Africa, and is rich in settler history and surrounded by lovely vineyards, orange orchards and wild flowers in spring in the near by Cederberg mountains you can view the many examples of Bushman rock art, and The Clanwilliam Dam is renowned as the best in the Western Cape for water skiing and also popular with anglers.

The rock paintings show that in days gone by, there were elephant, hippo and even rhino roaming the area. Sadly now all no longer.

When we arrived at Ndedema guest house, we were welcomed by the charming and friendly owners Johan and Wilma. After our suitcases were safely stored in our room, we both went for a swim in the pool in the garden.

The water in the pool that afternoon was 30°c, so you can imagine how hot it had been.

Johan soon joined us at the swimming pool for a chat. It is not often you meet someone who you instantly like, and who is so incredibly interesting and knowledgeable.

When we went back to our room to get ready for bed, Helen said "They are really nice people, and the garden is to die for, not to mention the room. Did you see there was a chocolate on each of our pillows, and rusks or as you call them beskuit, and other biscuits as well?"

"What do you mean; the garden is to die for?"

"There are so many different fruit trees, and everything is so green."

It had been a busy day, and yet another busy day waited for us in the morning.

Day 4

hile Helen slept, I went outside to listen to the birds and to enjoy an early morning coffee, and before long, Johan joined me for a chat, before he left for Cape Town. I was sad to see him go, and would have loved to have spent more time with him and learning from him.

Later that morning, we had breakfast next to the pool under some grape vines, with grape fruit, oranges and mango trees all around us, while Helen looked at our to do list.

Today it would be the rooibos factory, then on to a river feature known as hippo pools and after that a climb to view some rock paintings.

I was looking forward to visiting the rooibos factory, and I wasn't disappointed. During our first trip to the country, I had ordered 5 kilograms of Rooibos tea to take back to the UK, and this would be an opportunity to buy some more tea and other Rooibos products.

When we got to the factory, we were first shown a DVD on rooibos, where and how it was grown, and how it eventually became tea.

The factory also offered numerous other rooibos products from skin care products to salad dressings.

I was quite surprised to see that Helen even bought

some products, and was more surprised when she tried some rooibos tea.

"That's not like you Penguin" I said.

"What do you mean not like me?"

"Well Penguin, you never want any of my tea at home."

"No, but I had to try some at the factory, to see if it was any better than what you have at home."

Down the road from the rooibos factory was the leather shoe making factory, which was quite disappointing.

We popped back to the guest house to drop off our various rooibos products, and surprised and amused to find one of the staff ironing the sheets and pillow cases while still on the bed.

Next we were off to the tourism office to find out how to get to the hippo pools and rock paintings.

We wanted to know how far it was from Clanwilliam and what the road was like to get to them.

The person behind the desk assured us that it was a short journey by road. Well, some 80 kilometres along one of the worst gravel roads we had travelled on we finally reached the gate to the national park, and the entrance to the pool and rock paintings.

If she calls a journey of 80 kilometres short, I hate to imagine what she considers to be a long journey?

To visit the pools and paintings, we had to buy a permit.

Permits now purchased, we set off, and about 10 yards further, the car ground to a halt. Had we run out of petrol?

Helen first thought someone must have siphoned off the petrol while we were paying for the permit, or on second thoughts, could it be a faulty petrol gauge?

Walking back to the permit office Helen said "It is your fault."

"Why is it my fault? I had nothing to do with the car suddenly stopping."

"You said leave the windows open didn't you?"

"What has that got to do with no petrol?"

"How do you know someone has not opened the door and unlocked the petrol cap?"

"I don't know, but they would have had to be very quick. Any way, I don't think that is the problem."

"So bright spark, what is the problem?"

"I don't know, but I don't think that is the problem."

When we got back to the office, a rather disgruntled Helen explained what our problem was, and the really helpful clerk offered to check the car for us.

Well, after much banging and shaking of the car, he thought it might be better if we contacted the rental company.

We did, and were told it would take at least 3 or more hours before they could get a replacement car from Cape Town to us.

It was now almost 40°c, and apart from the office and some tres, there was not much shade to shelter in.

We went down to a stream which meandered its way through the park, and waited and waited and waited for the replacement car to arrive.

Finally the car arrived, and after asking directions to get back to Clanwilliam were given a much shorter route, which was mostly on a highway.

So much for the tourism office and their advice.

Finally back at the guest house in the replacement car, we went for a welcome swim and then got ready to enjoy a meal at one of the local restaurants.

Before leaving the UK, Johan and Wilma had told me about one of the locals, who made wall clocks from Ceder wood.

Apart from my love of rooibos, I also love natural wood. I had to get this unique clock.

Shortly before leaving for the restaurant, the man with the clock arrived.

In the town known as the rooibos centre you would expect and would not be disappointed to find out that the various chefs made maximum use of various rooibos infusions.

This included ice cream with rooibos, dips and sauces with rooibos, cakes and biscuits with rooibos, milk shakes with rooibos and even cocktails with rooibos.

I have been a rooibos tea lover for years, but Helen was put off with the amount of food and drinks with this plant in them.

We each had a steak, and Helen finished of the meal with a crème brulee infused with rooibos, while I had a slice of Cape brandy pudding topped with cream infused with rooibos, followed by a marula don pedro.

As she tucked in to her desert, I said "You see there is nothing wrong with that."

Helen didn't reply, but continued to eat her pudding.

"So was it that bad?"

Drinking her coffee, which didn't have any rooibos in it, she finally said "No, it wasn't bad at all, in fact really delicious."

Me and rooibos done for the day, it was back to the guest house and time to get ready for bed.

Day 5

The next morning after breakfast, we were on our way to Springbok some 350 kilometres away.

We were both sad to bid farewell to Wilma, and before leaving, stopped off at a florist and ordered some flowers to be delivered to her as a small thank you.

Springbok in the northern Cape is the largest town in the Namaqualand area and lies in a narrow valley between the high granite domes of the Klein Koperberge or Small Copper Mountains. Many years earlier, the town became the center in the region for copper mining.

The klipkoppie, a large bolder is the centre point of the town, with all the streets leading off from this landmark rock.

While the countryside up to and in and around Clanwilliam was lush and green, the closer we got to Springbok, the more bleak and desolate the land became.

Driving along the N7, Helen noticed strange circular rock formations dotted all over the place, as well as the almost leafless white coloured quiver tree, and then another plant which looked like beans hanging off it, just 2 of Namaqualand's many strange plants.

Each year after the winter rains, the arid surface erupts in a carpet of colour from thousands of flowers hidden in the dry dusty earth.

We arrived at Annie's cottage guest house in the afternoon. After Checking in, and chatting to the owner Petru, we decided it was time for a swim in the pool.

"That was the most boring stretch of road I have ever traveled cn"Helen said later.

"Why so?"

"Apart from rocks and the occasional plant, there was not much to see. It was just a flat and straight road."

Having enquired from Petru about places to eat, we made our way to a near by restaurant that night.

Day 6

The following day we had an early start. We had to be at our destination, the Orange River, 120 kilometres away by 9am.

The river is on the borders of South Africa and Namibia, and we had booked to do a few hours white water rafting on this mighty stretch of water.

Once again it was a straight and boring road. The landscape on the way to the border was no different from the road we had traveled on the day before; desolate with many rock formations, with strange looking Quiver trees and other small yellow shrubs being the only sign of life.

The quiver tree can live up to 400 years in this desert area and much like the baobab tree stores water in its trunk.

When we got to the border, we had to turn down a gravel road and travel about 10 kilometres to our final destination.

On arrival we met the guides. They had decided that Helen would go with one guide, and I with the other.

While we waited, we played with 2 dogs on the site, and soon after that, the guides gathered the rafts and put them on the back of a bakkie or pick up truck.

Then it was time to make our way down yet another gravel road next to the Orange River.

I sat in the front, while Helen stood in the back of the open bakkie.

She enjoyed the experience, but said this form of transport was not for her especially on a gravel road.

After reaching our launching point, the 2 rafts were unloaded and made ready for the water.

As we waited I said to Helen "now you know what it is like for many black people, and they have to do it every day and have no choice in the matter."

We each got in to and sat in our rafts with a guide each behind us.

On the journey down the river, Helen noticed what she thought were snakes in the water, but her guide reassured her that they were water birds, and from a distance when their long black necks appeared above the water they did look a bit like a snake.

Making her way down the river, she also saw herons, weaver birds, some cattle and sheep on either side of the bank, but sadly for her, no monkeys.

About 3 hours later, we reached the collection point. Helen was sitting in the water waiting for me.

After our pleasure trip down the river, Helen commented "I noticed there was more jaw than ore" coming from me.

I couldn't believe how warm the Orange River was in this area. The water was also not that clear, certainly nothing like the cold and clear waters found in the Drakensburg.

On our way back to springbok, we decided to visit a

typical Herero village with their round huts made out of Reads.

With time on our side, we also stopped at the Gogap nature reserve: with its outcrops of granite peaks as far as the eye could see, and many succulents only found in the area.

We were hoping to see springbok; gemsbok; the endangered Hartman's Zebra; the aardwolf; ostriches; black eagles; spotted dikkops and ground woodpeckers but sadly that didn't happen.

The only sign of life was a Gemsbok in the distance.

At the information centre, we met the on duty official, who you would have thought would be pleased to see some tourists, but this was not the case.

She appeared to be completely disinterested in us, and for that matter her job and surrounds.

Near the centre, we discovered and walked through the Hester Malan Wild Flower Garden with its selection of Namaqualand succulents.

We got to see the rare haunting halfmens ("halfperson" or Pachypodium namaquanum), which is only found in this area. These Tall, slender prehistoric plants are decorated with small leaves, and can grow up to 4 metres high.

The legend is the Nama, fleeing from the north, crossed the Orange River and longed to be back in their homeland.

Pitying them, God transformed them into these succulents so that they could look at the land of their origin forever.

The very top of the plant is usually bent and faces north towards Namibia. The tubular velvet-textured flowers appear from August to October and result in twin seedpods in a V-shape. These split down one side to release the wind-dispersed plumed seeds.

From a distance, the plant has the appearance of a person trudging up a slope from which its nickname and common name is "Halfmens."

Our visit to the nature reserve complete, it was now time to return to Springbok, find some where to eat that night, and get ready for the next leg of our journey.

We had already discovered that Springbok was not the venue for gourmet or a great variety of food.

Most of the restaurants were steak houses in one form or another.

When we got to the restaurant or steakhouse there was a large notice board with the names of those patrons, who had managed to eat a kilogram of steak in one sitting.

"Are you going to go for it?"

"Go for what?"

"I thought you would like your name on that board."

"You mean eat a kilogram of steak? I don't think so, but I will have a steak." Helen said.

I guess we should have known about the culinary delights on offer in the town. There was a large billboard just before we got to the town claiming Springbok was the beef capital.

Another interesting fact about Springbok which can not be verified but according to the owner of the guest house, there were no fleas in Springbok. She said it was too dry and too hot for them.

Day 7

Today would be the longest stretch for Helen to drive. From Springbok to Francschoek is about 570 kilometres.

The drive back along the N7 went by without incident apart from the inevitable road works with the 10 or 20 minute delays.

After about 400 kilometres we turned off the N7 and headed towards Citrusdal at the foot of the cederberg mountain range.

A further 30 kilometres off the N7 we reached the town. It was hot; we needed something cold to drink, and also to find somewhere to eat.

We decided to stop at the Replica of a pioneer cottage housing a coffee shop / deli / gift shop.

It was such a relief to sit inside and enjoy the air conditioning. The temperature outside was well over 42c, and it felt stifling.

"You know this is orange country." I said to Helen.

"Yes, I remember you telling me, but what about it?"

"I know you will probably want a cup of tea, but you cannot stop here and not have a freshly squeezed orange juice can you? If you don't, I am certainly going to have one." I said.

We both had the freshly squeezed orange juice and something to eat, before taking a walk through the gift shop, before resuming our journey.

"That orange juice was really divine, I am so glad I had it." Helen said.

The road to Franshoek would take us up and down mountains, over several bridges and passing numerous peach, pear, apple orchards and vineyards. The desolate landscape of Springbok was now replaced with lush green countryside.

"I do like this part of our journey. The scenery is really lovely." Helen said as she continued towards our next destination.

Finally we arrived in Franschoek, and drove through the small town looking for the Coach House, where we would be staying for 2 nights.

The building is over 100 years old, and also a national monument.

Minutes later we found the Coach House, parked outside it, and after meeting the owner Sharon, took our suitcases inside, and we then went for a swim.

We couldn't believe the guest house was only 50 metres from the Huguenot monument. We could walk there, but unfortunately, time was not on our side.

While sunning our selves next to the pool we got to meet Sharon's little Yorkshire terrier. Yet another friendly dog and owner.

That night, after asking Sharon where we could get a decent meal, we went to one of the many restaurants in the town.

Day 8

Franschoek is known as the food and wine capital of the country with its almost 30 restaurants, and as many wine cellars.

The town was originally called the Valley of the Huguenots, a community of French Huguenots, who were granted land in the valley by the Dutch government of the Cape, after fleeing their homeland when Protestantism was outlawed in France in 1685.

We woke up to a crystal clear Cape morning. Before breakfast, Helen had a look at the to do list. We had a busy schedule ahead of us.

First on the list was the Huguenot monument.

Helen with her French connection dating back some centuries wanted to visit the monument.

The Huguenot Memorial was inaugurated in 1948, and displays a female character with a broken chain in her left hand and a bible in her right. She is believed to represent the spirit of religious freedom, and the fleur-de-lis on her robe signifies noble spirit and character. Behind her are three arches, symbolic of the holy trinity and above that is the cross of the Christian faith. In front of the monument is a pond filled with water reflecting the colonnade behind it, an expression of tranquility of mind and spirit.

We sat on the lawns while Helen admired the view. At that time of the day, there were not that many visitors. The grounds were lovely and peaceful, and even better, it was not too hot.

"It is so peaceful. The grounds are lovely, and that view of the mountains in the distance is wonderful" she said while sitting on the bench and taking in the view.

"I am so glad you like it Penguin."

Next on the to do list that morning was another monument in Paarl, about 23 kilometres away. We were headed for the "Taal" or language monument.

This monument on a hilltop over looking Paarl is dedicated to the Afrikaans language and was opened in 1975. It charts the course of the language and at the time it was opened celebrated 50 years since it was declared an official language of South Africa separate from Dutch.

At the beginning of the monument is a plaque, with 2 poems written in Afrikaans, and as you make your way up this language tribute, various rounded and hollow structures symbolize political developments in the country, as well as the influence of different languages and cultures on Afrikaans.

6 pillars symbolize different stages of Afrikaans development. The first is called (clear west), a tribute to the European heritage, then (Magical Africa), the African influences on the language, followed by (Bridge), the link between Europe and Africa, (Afrikaans), representing the language itself, (Republic), the declaration in 1961

and finally (Malay) and how that language and culture influenced Afrikaans.

Concerts and events are sometimes held at an open stadium at the bottom of the monument.

After walking up and through the monument, we stopped at the gift and coffee shop to have a drink, before driving on to Paarl itself.

While walking around the town, Helen found this most amazing ice cream shop selling 85% pure chocolate ice cream.

"We have to go into this shop."

"What shop is this?"

"It's a surprise, but I know you will love it" Helen said as we entered the shop.

Helen knew apart from biltong, I could eat ice cream any time of the day and night. Naturally we had to try or rather I had to try one or two, especially their chocolate and orange, which was wonderful.

Driving around the area, Helen couldn't help but be in awe at the sites of mountains, streams, vineyards and orchards.

Back at the guesthouse, we once again went for an afternoon swim.

We decided not to eat at one of the restaurants that night, but to buy some snacks and something to drink, and to make our way up to the top of the Franschoek pass, to watch the sun go down.

The pass is one of the most scenic drives in the area,

and much to Helen's delight as we made our way to the top baboons appeared from no where on the side of the road.

All the rubbish bins at the various viewing areas had baboon safe locks, which prevented these animals from opening and trashing them.

I mockingly said to Helen "I don't know why I bothered suggesting watching the sun go down, when you are more taken in with the sight of those baboons."

Once the sun had completely faded, we made our way back down, and after stopping for a coffee, went back to the guest house after which bed called.

Day 9

After breakfast and saying hello and goodbye to the yorkie and Sharon, it was time to pack our bags and head off via Stellenbosch to Hermanus some 100 kilometres away for one night.

En route we stopped off at one of the local markets held on a vineyard, which was extremely poor with not much on offer.

When we got in to the car, we noticed our shoes were covered in these really sharp little thorns, and I don't mean just a few, but scores attached to each shoe.

I wouldn't be too wrong if I said that the thorns were the highlight of that market.

Thorns now off our shoes and swept out of the car and 60 kilometres later, we arrived in Hermanus to find our next guesthouse.

Hermanus was originally called Hermanuspietersfontein, but shortened because the name was too long for the postal service.

The town is about 110 kilometres from Cape Town and there is much debate whether the garden route starts here or in the city.

Something else which makes the town some what unique is its historic railway station building without a railway line. The founders of the town decided not to lay any tracks as this would have made Hermanus more commercial and they felt that it needed to stay a small Fisherman's Village.

It also boasts with the world's only Whale Crier; thousands of people flock to the town each year to watch the Wales from the numerous cliffs and viewing platforms.

There is an annual whale festival at the end of every September to celebrate the return of the southern white whale.

We were met by the owners and their 2 westies. The couple and the 2 dogs showed us to our room.

The hosts and their 2 dogs were lovely. However, I think the owner's wife had a drinking problem.

While we enjoyed the swimming pool, she sat on a pool-side chair enjoying a bottle or 2 of whine and her words became slowly more and more slurred.

After the quick swim and a pool-side chat, we were off to Harold Porter Botanical Gardens near Bettys Bay. Included in the gardens are four vegetation types that occur naturally in the Overberg. They are forests, wetlands, coastal dunes and fynbos, featuring Proteas, Ericas, Restios and leucadendrons.

I joked with Helen calling her a spoilsport.

"Why am I a spoilsport?"

"I am sure our hostess wanted you to join her in a bottle of wine."

"She was a bit strange." Helen admitted.

The walkways in the gardens lead across bridges until finally reaching the waterfalls. There are many picnic areas with benches to sit on.

While baboons, leopard, Porcupines, genets, mongooses, otters, and dassies inhabit the gardens, we unfortunately or fortunately; depending on which animal did not see any.

After retracing our steps we took a look around the small book and curio shop, and found a tray with various local birds painted on it.

In the evening we went to Annie se Kombuis, one of the local restaurants claiming to serve true South African food.

We settled for the platter for two. This would give Helen the chance to try a selection of various South African dishes.

The restaurant was rather stuffy inside, so we decided to sit outside, wanting some fresh air. However, the tables were in an alley way; not a very inspiring setting, or very pleasant view.

The food was bland and average, and the portions hardly enough to feed one person, let alone two people.

The meager offering included a fish dish called smoorsnoek, or smoked barracouta, Skilpadjies, (Tortoise), the name given to this liver delicacy from its shape. Other dishes to share were ostrich neck stew, bobotie, springbok tart, venison and chicken pies, pap, pumpkin fritters, Green Bean and Potato Stew.

Helen tried their malva pudding, while I had the Van

Der Hum ice cream with naartjie sauce; a great idea and well worth the visit, if only for this delicious desert.

I guess for any tourist, not knowing better, it would have been satisfactory, but I was more than disappointed.

If I had an Afrikaans aunty (tannie), I am sure she would have walked out in disgust.

Before I continue, the recipes for these dishes and all other South African dishes mentioned in this book can be found at the back of the book.

By the time we got back, we forgot our room did not have air conditioning, so we slept with the windows open. Helen was extremely nervous, thinking burglars might suddenly appear even though the windows were all barred.

At breakfast the next morning we met a German golfer, who told us it was his 15th time staying at the guesthouse. I guess he didn't mind the hostess drinking too much every now and again.

Day 10

Even before we set out on this trip, Helen had decided she wanted to revisit Prince Albert, about 400 kilometres away.

On our previous visit to the Cape and oudtshoorn, she had fallen in love with the village.

Before we got to Prince Albert, we visited Botlierskop Private Game Reserve, about 30 kilometres outside Mossel bay.

The 270 Kilometre stretch of road between Hermanus and Mossel bay was uneventful. We had been down the N2 on our last trip, and there was nothing new.

We stopped at Spur steak ranch Mossel Bay for lunch; aned before leaving for the game reserve, Helen ordered a takeaway pizza from Panarottis to have for dinner that night.

When we arrived at the game reserve and paid for our tickets, we waited to climb on board the 4x4 along with several other passengers.

Sitting at the back of the vehicle gave us a great vantage point. Our guide was very good stopping and pointing out to his passengers the types of animals, their habits and any other unique qualities.

We were lucky, we saw the rare black Impala, Rhino, Buffalo in the distance, Giraffe, Mountain Zebra, Eland, wildebeest, the multi coloured bontabok, waterbuck, kudu, Elephants and not forgetting the leopard tortoise.

After the game reserve, we changed vehicles and made our way in to the Lion Sanctuary, with its 3 lions.

The enclosure is cordoned off from the rest of the reserve.

Helen said she felt quite nervous when one of the lions fixed his stare on her.

Jokingly I said "How do you think the lion felt?"

"What do you mean?"

"How do you think the lion felt when you were staring back at him?"

I don't know which was more exciting for Helen, the animals or the 4x4 drive. She said she loved every lump and bump in the road during our 3 and a half our drive.

Next time, I might have to forget about viewing animals but find a 4x4 track for her to drive on.

With the thrills of the bumpy ride behind us, we left for Prince Albert some 140 kilometres away.

By the time we got to Dennehof guest house, a former farm, it was almost 8pm and the temperature was still 27c.

Ria, the owner was their to greet us, and after being shown our room, Helen and I settled down to enjoy a pizza and biltong, and relax until bed time.

Helen's only concern about the room; it was an old converted barn and there might be according to her, rain spiders.

Day 11

Prince Albert is on the southern edge of the Great Karoo, under the foot of the Swartberg Mountains.

The name Karoo comes from Karusa, a Khoi word which means dry, barren, thirstland.

The town was founded in 1762on the loan farm De Queek Vallei with Zacharias De Beer, its first owner.

It was first known as Albertsburg, but renamed Prince Albert in honour of Queen Victoria's consort.

Visitors can find many well-preserved Cape Dutch, Karoo and Victorian buildings, thirteen of which are National Monuments. There are several olive farms and other very large export fruit farms in the area, as well as sheep farms, an export mohair trade, and each year the village celebrates the well-known olive festival.

There are also numerous succulents only found in this area.

In the morning after a cup of coffee, Helen spent time in the spa bath on the patio outside our room before making our way down to the garden for breakfast.

The tables were set out on a sun deck under trees and next to a small stream, and while having breakfast, we met the owners 2 dogs.

Now nourished, we went in to town and looked around the many curio type shops in the main street. However, and most importantly, I managed to find a butchery, and replenished my biltong supply.

The high street and butchery now taken care of, we visited a local dairy, which was disappointing. There was not much we had not seen or tasted before.

From the dairy we drove 25 kilometres to an olive farm.

This was far more interesting. The owner told us how olives were grown, picked and pressed, and then we got to taste the different types of olives.

We both love olives, and bought quite a lot of products with olives in them.

From the olive farm, we made our way back to town to one of the few tea rooms named the Lazy Lizard.

There can't be that many tea rooms which started as a bus terminal, then a curio shop and finally the most wonderful tea room.

Naturally being in the Karoo, you would expect them to serve various lamb dishes, which they did.

Helen chose the lamb sandwich with mint and olive paste, while I had a lamb pie. Both were delicious.

We couldn't resist the freshly baked apple pie with cream from one of the farms and a milk tart and home made lemonade.

The owner lives opposite the Lazy Lizard, and bakes and cooks each morning before the tea room opens its doors.

Another plus as far as Helen was concerned; dog owners were allowed to sit outside with their pets.

In the afternoon I spent the time in the swimming pool at the guest house, while Helen went for a beauty treatment.

By the time she got back at about 5pm the temperature had cooled down to 39 c, and soon after Helen joined me in the pool.

While splashing around and cooling down in the pool, we met some people from Hermanus, who were visiting the village for a few days.

After we all put the country to right, I discovered they knew a couple of my former editors. Once this had been established, we had even more to talk about.

About 2 hours later, it was time to get out of the pool and find some where to eat. The owners had recommended a restaurant in the high street.

When we got to the Gallery Café as it is called, we discovered one of the many dishes was a choice of Springbok or Warthog carpaccio, which I chose. Helen tried some, but wasn't too keen on the game. She settled on Karoo shank of lamb.

After the meal we chatted to Brent, the chef and owner of the restaurant, who promised if we returned the next night he would get more game.

At about 9.30pm we returned to the guesthouse and you would think the temperature would now begin to cool down, but no, it was still 32c.

Day 12

The next morning after breakfast and playing with the dogs for a while, we were off to visit a fig farm.

Unfortunately it was not as interesting as the olive farm the previous day, but we did buy a few fig products before returning to the town.

"Shall we go and have a cup of tea or coffee?"

"You can have tea, but I am going to have iced coffee." I said.

As we sat outside drinking our tea and iced coffee, Helen saw and chatted to the beauty therapist from the day before, and later we met Brent the chef from the previous night. He assured us, he would get some different game in that night.

Helen was already beginning to feel like one of the locals.

"I really like this town. We haven't been here more than 24 hours, and I already feel part of the community. Everyone is so friendly."

"Penguin, they might be, but remember what small town gossip is like." I reminded her.

"That's true, but I still love this place."

"Any way, forget about gossip, are you going to have something to eat?"

"I think I might be tempted."

"What are you going to have?"

"I think I am going to try that apple pie you had yesterday."

"Good idea!! Me too."

While we sat and savored the apple pie, it was nice to see Helen so happy. I don't know if it was the air, the scenery or just the town, but she was happy, and it really didn't matter why.

Back at the guest house, the afternoon was spent in and out of the pool until it was time to return to the restaurant.

The chef had kept his promise. On the menu were Kudu and Blue wildebeest steaks. How lucky I was.

When we arrived at the restaurant that night, the waitress had brought her dog with her, so I spent time sitting on the floor with the dog. As had happened on our previous visit, Helen was embarrassed about me sitting on the floor in the middle of a restaurant. But, I did point out to her; no one else had yet arrived at the restaurant.

I enjoyed the game Brent had cooked, while Helen loved the lamb shank.

At the end of the evening, we spent another hour chatting to the chef, who like us loved theatre, and had spent some time in London, and who had also seen many of the shows we had seen.

A quick 5 minute drive back to the guest house, and off to bed. We had a long day ahead of us tomorrow.

Day 13

After the call of the hadeda, a cup of coffee, a shower then breakfast, it was time to leave and drive the 380 kilometres to our next resort. At least our journey would take us on the R62, which claims to be the longest whine route in the world.

This scenic route takes you through and over mountains and valleys passing streams, orchards and many different farms.

Between Prince Albert and Rawsonville where our next guest house was situated, the countryside was dotted with numerous game and nature reserves.

The first town after Prince Albert and Oudtshoorn was Calitzdorp, bordered on 3 sides by mountains. This town is in the Klein Karoo or small Karoo. It is a bit of a contradiction with some parts desert-like and other parts extremely fertile and green. The town is best known for its port.

The next town was Ladismith.

The area produces a third of all the apricots and plums in the country and also has a thriving grape and whine industry. It is also known for its 2 cheese factories.

We didn't need an excuse to stop and see if the factory had any unusual cheese or dairy products.

Unfortunately it did not have any thing unusual and the factory mainly produces for the big retail trade.

Once again Ladismith, like many of the towns on the R62 were flanked by mountains.

In Ladismith there is a story that the peak of the so-called magic mountain or Towerkop, which rises over the town, was said to have been struck by a witch in anger because it blocked her way over the mountain. The result was a deep split at the top of the mountain, leaving two perfect halves.

Some 76 kilometres further on was Barrydale.

The town of Barrydale lies at the foot of the Langeberge in the heart of the Tradouw Valley and lies on the border between the Cape Overberg and the succulent Klein Karoo. The all year round climate is perfect for growing apples, pears, oranges, apricots, figs, peaches and there are grape farms scattered across the valley.

The area has the best of both worlds; the summer is ripe with fruit, while autumn is the beginning of the protea season, and in winter aloes, milkbush, concertina plant and other succulents begin flowering.

After walking around the town, we went to Clark of the Karoo with its landmark windmill outside it.

The restaurant claims to offer traditional Karoo dishes. It also had a shop selling home produce.

Helen ordered a lamb bobotie while I ordered Karoo lamb chops.

While we waited for our meal to arrive, we sat outside enjoying the fresh air and the tranquility found in small towns.

"I don't know why, but I much prefer this town to Prince Albert" I said to Helen.

"How can you say that?"

"I know we haven't seen much of the town, but firstly, I prefer the weather. It is not as humid and secondly it is closer to Cape Town."

"Why do you want to be close to Cape Town?"

"At least it is not that far to go if we wanted to go to theatre or any other live performance."

"Yes I guess you are right about that, but I still prefer Prince Albert."

The bobotie was fine, but I found the lamb chops tough and not very tender or succulent.

The next few towns we drove through were Montagu, Ashton, Bonnievale and McGregor.

We Stopped at Robertson to fill up with petrol and to take a look around at a couple of farm stalls, but didn't find anything or any product that unusual.

At about 5pm that afternoon, we eventually arrived at Rawsonville and before finding our way to the guest house looked for a supermarket to buy some provisions during our stay.

The only shop open was a foreign owned mini store.

While trying to avoid standing on the local resident, a cat, we bought some milk and a few other goodies.

When we reached the farm, we were greeted by Sally the owner.

It soon became obvious the owner's claims about the resort via the internet were not the case in reality.

Yes, it might very well have been a "working whine farm", but, the "Friendly hosts will give you a warm welcome and happily show you around their farm and vineyards" did not happen.

I would certainly not call our welcome warm, nor the owner particularly friendly and the offer to be shown around the farm never materialized.

Another claim which was not true was "A 5 minute walk from the cottages is a gorgeous secluded mountain pool."

Yes, it was 5 minutes away; if you knew where it was, and when we finally found it, the "mountain pool", turned out to be a slime ridden rock pool of water.

The 3 "white-washed cape cottages" might have been white washed, but I think in years gone by, they were used as servant quarters.

The furniture was cheap, carpets thread-bare, and the bed without sheets.

When we got to the guest house, we asked about the rock pool, and Sally waved her hand presumably in its general direction.

We first unpacked, and then began the walk up the so-called mountain to find the pool. 20 minutes later, we had still not found the rock pool.

I said to Helen I would wait while she went up ahead and tried to find it.

Later after about 30 minutes, an exasperated, disgruntled and hot Helen returned not having found the "rock pool."

We slowly made our way back to the room, to decide what to do next.

When we got back to the cottage, Helen retired to the bedroom, while I sat outside.

I knew she was stressed and in a bad mood, and it would be better to leave her alone while she calmed down.

I also knew that her first response would be to say "Let's just leave and go down to Cape Town, and to hell with this place."

After about 15 minutes I knocked on the door, and found Helen stretched out on the bed.

I was right. Her first words to me were

"Let's just leave and go down to Cape Town, and to hell with this place."

When I pointed out that we had already paid for this dump, and to leave now would mean spending more money. We could hardly expect a refund.

She finally agreed, and we decided to make the best of a bad situation.

To make matters worse, on entering the room, Helen discovered spiders running up and down all four walls.

As she has this fear of spiders, it was decided to move

the bed in to the middle of the floor and away from the 4 walls.

With the temperature in the high 30s we also discovered there was no air conditioning, and searching through all the cupboards, eventually we managed to find a small fan.

The windows did not have burglar bars on them either, so Helen refused to sleep with the windows open in case of unwanted visitors in the night, be they burglars, spiders or any other uninvited animal or insect.

It was hell that night.

Before hell that night, we decided to have a barbecue. The barbecue area was about 15 metres away from the cottage. There was also no firewood.

Reverting back to ancient times, I sent Helen out to gather some kindle and bits of wood.

Thanks to the help of a candle we managed to eventually get a fire going, and enjoy our barbecue.

The patio did not have any chairs on it, so we were forced to perch on the walls and eat our food.

During the night Helen thought she heard sounds of an animal outside, and was not able to have a peaceful sleep.

Day 14

In the morning we left for Worcester, found some where to stop and have breakfast, and made our way back to my old school for a guided tour.

Parts of the old school still remained, but in the passing years, much had changed with new additions to classrooms and hostels.

Health and safety was now the name of the game. Occupational therapists and permanent nursing staff were now the order of the day. Written permission was needed from the parents before any child could set foot in the town.

The school might have changed its name to the pioneer school for the blind, but the pioneering spirit had gone.

After the tour of the school, we went to Kleinplassie, a living open air and cultural history museum on the outskirts of the town.

Visitors can watch how the locals in days gone by Rolled tobacco, baked bread in an outside oven, made soap and candles, and a blacksmith demonstrated metal work. There were also Donkey cart rides available for kids.

The farm yard concentrates on agricultural and home industries.

When we got there, we were greeted by chickens roaming freely, which surprisingly took little interest in us.

I guess they must be used to visitors.

We walked around looking at the various old rooms from bedrooms to kitchens and living areas. We also saw many different implements used at home and for every day living.

Instead of going back to Worcester for lunch, we decided to try out the restaurant at the museum.

This was very relaxing as we sat outside with the sound of chickens clucking all around us.

After lunch we made our way back to the guest house. We were determined today to find this elusive rock pool.

Fortunately for us, when we set out to find it, we met another couple on their way down from the pool, who gave us directions how to get there, but they did say not to expect much.

They were right. It was a slimy rock pool, if you could call it a rock pool.

Clambering over rocks we made it to the pool. We stood in the water for awhile, before making our way back to the cottage.

One more night to go in this hell hole Helen said as we went back in to Worcester to find a restaurant that night.

Once again not knowing the town, it was a question of finding any restaurant chain. I am sure there are probably some nice restaurants in Worcester, but where?

We settled on Panarottis.

It would be an early start the next day, so we packed our bags ready to leave the next morning.

Day 15

At 5am after a quick cup of coffee we left for Cape Town, and to visit Robben Island.

We had to be at the Waterfront before 9am to purchase tickets and to board the ferry to the once infamous and now famous and world heritage site Robben Island.

I don't have to tell you, for years it was the home of formerly imprisoned leader Nelson Mandela and many other political activists.

The name is Dutch for "seal island", and they were the first settlers to use this oval shaped island as a prison.

Later, the British used the island for political prisoners and it also served as a leper colony and animal quarantine station.

During the Second World War 6 and 9 inch guns were erected on it to defend Cape Town.

The waters of the island are a graveyard to many ships thanks to the rough seas that pound the island.

Jan van Riebeeck, the founder of Cape Town commanded his troops to light huge bonfires each night at the top of Fire Hill, now Minto Hill to warn ships of the rocks that surround the island.

On the ferry you might be lucky to see Cape Fur Seals, Whales and Dolphins, and on the island small herds of Bontebok, Springbok, Steenbok, Fallow Deer and Eland.

Our plan was to stop some where en route and have breakfast, but the closer we got to Cape Town the busier the traffic got, the slower our progress, and the less time we had.

We had forgotten about the early morning rush hour, as workers went along to their offices shops and factories.

At 8.45am we arrived and parked the car, and made a dash for the ticket office, had it been 3 minutes later, we would have missed the ferry.

"We were so lucky finding that parking, and even more lucky to find someone who knew the way to the booking office." Helen said.

The trip took 30 minutes and the sound of the engines in the water was drowned out by the sound of the excited tourists most of whom were on their cell phones.

Reaching the Island, we disembarked and boarded a couple of coaches ready to leave for the tour.

The tour guide first introduced her self to the passengers before beginning her talk about the island and its former inmates.

When the coach reached the quarry where Mandela had previously dug out and broke up the lime stone rocks, it stopped and the guide allowed passengers to take pictures.

Noticing I was blind, she offered to take me and Helen to exactly where Mandela had been forced to work for so many of those years.

When the 3 of us left the coach, and walked to the cave

where Mandela and others had worked, Helen was quite embarrassed as the coach load of passengers looked on.

Walking back to the coach, I picked up a couple of the lime stones, which you never know might have been the same stones broken by Mandela him self.

After the brief excursion, we continued our trip as we made our way to the jail.

Here we were introduced to another guide, a former inmate, who took over the job of explaining what happened to him and other activists during those years of incarceration, and what prison life was like.

During our tour of the prison block, he too was extremely kind and thoughtful, and unlocked the door which housed Mandela so I could walk inside and find out how small the cell actually was.

I didn't know until much later, that not many people are ever allowed into the cell.

One other person, who I know shared the same space with me, even though not at the same time was President Obama.

I couldn't believe how small the cell was, and to think Mandela spent almost 18 years in this cell.

One other thing which astounded and ashamed me, was finding out how the different racial groups received different portions of food.

Indian prisoners received the most, followed by coloured, and finally the black inmates, who received the least.

I couldn't understand how any human being could treat people like that. How the Afrikaner government could call themselves Christians? Mind you, the Dutch Reform church which most Afrikaners belonged to also supported apartheid.

Once we finished our tour of the prison, we all made our way to the harbor and boarded the ferry for the trip back to the waterfront.

The time was now almost 1pm, and we still had not had anything to eat, but there was no time to waste.

This was our penultimate day in the country and we had a couple of appointments to keep.

Next on our itinerary was to meet up with a couple who made Armenian specialty chocolates.

I thought the visit would be completed in about 10minutes, but how wrong this meeting would prove to be.

When we arrived at the house, we were invited in, and after about 15 minutes offered a cup of coffee.

Our host Robert, then proceeded to open a container full of coffee beans, and for the next 15 minutes sat and slowly ground them by hand.

30 minutes later, we were still waiting for the coffee and chocolates to appear.

When the coffee did finally arrive, to our dismay, it was in 2 of the smallest cups known to man.

At this stage, there was still no sign of the chocolates.

Once again about 30 minutes later, a plate of the

specialty chocolates appeared, and our hosts insisted that we sample them.

By this stage we could have eaten a horse or for that matter, any animal which might appear in the garden or in the house.

The intended quick visit to buy some of the chocolate, was rapidly becoming an ordeal. I kept on saying to Helen that we had to go as we would be late for another appointment.

My comments seemed to go unnoticed. Was she waiting for the chocolates, or was she just being extra polite?

Two hours after we first arrived, we finally left, with Helen having placed an order to be collected the next day.

Beware any animals I thought, I might eat you.

An entire afternoon had been wasted just for a few chocolates, which were no better than other specialty shops might have offered.

We drove back to Bret and Sharon in Fish Hoek, said hello to them and the dogs, went for a quick swim, before getting ready to find a restaurant and then on to the Fugard theatre to see one of his plays.

In desperation we stopped at the first restaurant which happened to be a Chinese restaurant.

The food can only be described as average, but beggars can't be choosers. We had to be at the theatre in the middle of Cape Town at 6.30pm to collect the tickets.

Finally had something to eat, we made our way to the theatre.

However, Helen did not enjoy the performance. So much for me wanting her to enjoy a Fugard production.

Back to the cottage that night, to make sure we had packed everything.

The next day, we would be leaving Cape Town on our way back to the UK.

Day 16

We woke to yet another beautiful summer Cape morning, and after saying goodbye to Bret, Sharon and the dogs we drove to Canal Walk for a final look around and buy those last minute or forgotten presents.

After lunching at the mal, we went to pick up the chocolates.

This time, I decided to wait in the car with an imaginary headache, which meant Helen would collect, and pay for the chocolates, and make her excuses as to why she could not stay, especially if they offered to make her a cup of coffee.

Cape Town International Airport here we come.

I must say I was incredibly disappointed at the SAA business class lounge at the airport. Compared to Heathrow, it was pathetic.

Waiting to take off, I asked Helen would she like to come back again, and perhaps see other parts of the country.

She said "yes, the more I see of the country the more I like it. If it wasn't for the crime and corruption would happily move here tomorrow."

On the way back flying high over the African skies, while Helen watched a couple of movies, I thought where we could next go.

Yes, there were many sites we had not seen in the Cape, but also elsewhere. Hopefully, there would be another time to enjoy and explore the country.

Journey 3

Drakensberg discontent

Third time lucky so the saying goes, but this trip to South Africa would not be lucky or that enjoyable. If things could go wrong, they would and they did.

In the months after our previous trip, my hip joint had got gradually worse. If I had not been on strong pain killers I would not have been able to walk from one room to another.

Not with standing the hip problem, it was back to the internet and first on the agenda would be to find a reasonably priced flight.

Our 2 previous trips had been in January and early February. It was time for Helen to experience a different season.

We settled for September, having found reasonably priced tickets with Emirates.

Another reason to fly with this airline for the first time

was the chance to spend a day and night in Dubai; a city both of us had not previously visited.

Our first trip had taken us briefly through Durban, and then on to the north of the province. This time it would be a visit to the Drakensberg Mountains and a longer stay in Durban.

During that first visit to the country, all Helen got to see of Durban were the highways after we landed at the city's King Shaka airport, when we collected the car and headed for St Lucia.

The day of departure soon arrived. Our dogs were in safe keeping thanks to her parent's baby sitting them again.

Setting off from home, we arrived about 3 hours later at Gatwick in London.

We had planned to meet up with Tracey, Helens sister at the airport.

Getting out of the car in London, I suddenly realised with a sinking feeling I had left my wallet with credit cards and some money in it back in Wales.

When I told Helen, she first thought I was joking, but soon changed her mind, when she saw how pale I had suddenly become.

I blamed this blunder on the fact I had spent so much time making sure her parents knew exactly what food to give the dogs, to make sure they had water, when to walk them, along with an A4 page of instructions.

There was no time to drive back to Wales to collect my

wallet. The first problem would be trying to collect the money I had pre-ordered for collection at Gatwick. No doubt proof and presentation of the card would be required.

As I am not known for my diplomacy, I left it to Helen to plead and beg the bank officials at the airport to hand over the cash.

For once I remained silent as she spoke and explained the situation to various officials.

Finally after calling and consulting various managers, they gave us our money.

The first problem and hurdle out of the way, it was now time to think about how to get my wallet.

Tracey offered to liaise with her parents and to have the wallet couriered out to South Africa.

The time had come to say goodbye and make our way to the aircraft. We would now have to wait until we got to Dubai to make further arrangements during our 4 hour stopover.

Fortunately I had bought a mini tablet to take out to Kit my brother's girlfriend, and this would now come in handy at the airport. Helen would be able to email Tracey and contact anyone else.

Before I continue with our sorrowful tale I must comment on Emirates airline. The cabin crew were extremely efficient, friendly, and what astounded me unlike most airlines which could only communicate in 2 or 3 different languages, their crew named about 14 different languages.

After disembarking, and making our way through the vast terminal we settled down to wait text, email and phone while planning our next move.

With Helen busy on the tablet, I contacted my bank via the UK, and was told it would cost me £100 to replace my card, if I reported it stolen.

The more I tried to explain my situation, the more minutes were ticking by on the phone card I had purchased after landing.

Finally I decided it wasn't worth £100, but instead to allow Tracey to have my wallet or cards sent out to South Africa.

Decision made, we then waited to board our next flight at 4am Dubai time arriving in Johannesburg at 11am that morning.

Day 1

As you can well imagine, Helen and I had a rather restless night, all the time worrying about when and how we would be reunited with my bank cards.

Flying over Johannesburg and about to land, I also remembered I had in my distant wallet the card Helen used to book and pay for the hire car, and no doubt they would also want to see her credit card.

When we landed, we had to wait almost one hour until a suitable walkway was found to park the plane at.

We were finally allowed into the terminal, after what seemed like hours, and collected our suitcases and made our way to the car rental company.

Fortunately for us, a passport and the confirmation letter was all that was required.

Suitcases in the boot and a full tank of petrol we left the airport at about 1pm heading towards Howick in KwaZulu-Natal some 450 kilometres away.

This would be the first time Helen would experience the N3, one of the busiest highways in the country. At any time of day or night hundreds of heavy laden trucks make their way in both directions between Johannesburg and Durban.

Between the various tolls, we would first pass the townships of Katlehong and Vosloorus then Heidelberg,

Villiers, Harrismith, Van Reenen's Pass, Ladysmith, Estcourt. Mooi River and finally the turn off to Howick.

Our first stop would be at the top of Van Reenen pass for a quick cup of tea and something to eat, before taking Helen to see the small chapel with only eight seats in it, and built by a father in memory of his son. The church claimed to be the smallest Roman Catholic Church in the world.

We had to make several more stops before reaching Howick to allow Helen to rest her eyes and to drink cups of coffee.

If the monotony of the road, and her overtiredness were not bad enough, the weather was closing in on us, and each time we were forced to stop, it was getting later and later and darker and darker.

Helen later described the journey to Howick as horrendous and one of the worst she had ever undertaken. She had not slept for 36 hours, and found the drive down the highway mind-numbing.

A journey which would normally take about 4 hours took us almost 6, but we finally found the guest house and with gentle rain falling made our way to the room.

After unpacking, we went into the town to find any restaurant for a quick meal, and the first we found was a Portuguese restaurant.

A quick meal and an early night followed.

Day 2

Howick and the surrounding area are known as the place of many waterfalls. The original Zulu inhabitants called it The Place of the Tall One with the water falling 95 metres down in to a deep pool.

Visitors can view the falls from virtually the middle of the town, and once finished admiring these falls there are several others including the 25 metre Cascade Falls and the 37 metre Shelter Falls. While 15 minutes way are the 105 metre Karkloof Falls.

Previously renowned visitors to the town included Mark Twain, and later Nelson Mandela, who was arrested in the neighborhood. Howick now has a monument to acknowledge this.

The Drakensberg mountain range in KwaZulu-Natal is home to 17 of the highest peaks in Southern Africa, with such alluring names as Champagne and Giants Castle, Trojan Wall, Rhino Peak and Devil's Knuckles.

When we woke up the following morning, the weather had not changed much and during that day, the temperature did not get much above 9c. But at least I got to hear the hadeda.

While the countryside was supposed to be lovely and green and remind visitors of England, it certainly wasn't like that when we were there. It was the end of winter, and the beginning of spring, and the countryside was brown and parched.

Helen kept on saying she would have been warmer in the UK and didn't know why she had come all the way just to be rained on. She had not packed any warm clothes or an umbrella.

Thanks to 2 lovely friendly Scotty dogs, they helped to cheer Helen up.

At breakfast served in the dining room that morning we met Stuart and Rieva, a couple from Durban. The 4 of us spent about one hour just chatting, before we made our separate ways for the day.

This was one of those chance meetings, where one instantly liked and got on with each other.

Apart from the waterfall, it was time to see what the 80 kilometre Midlands Meander had to offer with its array of local artists: potters, weavers, woodcrafters, leather and metal workers, box makers, herb growers, cheese makers, beer brewers and many more art and craft shops.

Once again, luck was not on our side. Many of the shops that day were closed, but we did get to view some of the craft work and also stopped at one of the well known local brewers. This micro set up stocked beers with such names as whistling weasel, pie-eyed possum, pickled pig porter' and a tiddly toad lager.

The weather continued to be wet cold and misty through out the day, which didn't make Helen feel happy or glad to be back in the country.

"Why have I come all the way here to put up with typically English weather? I haven't got any warm clothes, nor a rain coat or even umbrella."

To say Helen was feeling miserable would be an understatement.

Even though the weather was not kind to us, we or rather I had a nice day out, and when we got back were greeted by 2 little dogs.

I think the highlight for Helen that day was the 2 dogs.

That evening we dined at a local Portuguese restaurant, before returning to the guest house.

Day 3

When we woke up the next morning, we began to wonder if we were still in the UK. The weather had not changed; it was still dull, rainy and misty.

Today after breakfast, we were on our way to the valley of a thousand hills and to a restaurant which boasted incredible views of the surrounding landscape.

At breakfast we met up with Stuart and Rieva again and immediately struck up a conversation almost as if we had known each other for years.

2 Hours later we said our goodbyes to our new found friends, and it was time to pack up and leave.

The plan was to stop and have lunch in the valley of a thousand hills, then on to meet my brother Kit and his Thai girlfriend at their house in Durban North.

Any ideas of our luck changing today were quickly dashed. When we got to the car, we discovered we had a flat tire.

Helen phoned the rental company, who said they would send a replacement car and asked us to wait.

Well, we waited, and waited and waited, but no replacement car.

Finally Helen went to the office to tell them about our problem, but the owners didn't seem to care.

The young receptionist, who was sitting in her office

next door, heard us talking, and when Eve and Roland failed to help came outside and said she had asked her partner to drive across to us and he would help.

With in minutes of arriving, he replaced the tire, and we were on our way.

We offered to pay him, but he refused to take any money.

Driving down to Durban I once again thought the internet did not tell the whole story.

According to the Howick guest house blurb "We hope that guests will recognize and enjoy the warmth and welcoming ambience that comes from generations of hosts who enjoyed welcoming strangers to the farm and having them depart as friends, just as we do today."

All I can say to this is that owners in days gone by might have been warm and welcoming, but we and certainly another couple who we met and became friends with did not experience these attributes.

Eve and her partner Roland could not be bothered in the least, and in fact, I don't think we ever got to meet the person called Roland.

Any way enough of these people who appear to be in tourism only to line their pockets. Pity they do not consider customer service as part of tourism.

The room had been lovely, and the 2 Scotty dogs made up for the lack of friendliness by their Owners.

Take 2 and we were ready to go once again.

Our first stop would be a coffee plantation, but you guessed it, we couldn't find it, and when we phoned the owners, they told us our satnav had taken us to their house and not to the plantation.

By this time the weather was even gloomier, with visibility down to about 10 metres.

"Penguin, let's forget about the coffee, and make our way to the restaurant" I said.

Helen, who was not in a good mood, reluctantly agreed.

The journey from Howick had taken us up and down hills and this continued until we got to the restaurant at Botha's hill.

While the restaurant boasts about its stunning views over the valley, this was certainly not the case the day we were there.

For once, we could not blame the owner or the internet. There was nothing he or we could do, so we sat inside enjoyed our meal and left for Durban North.

Helen's mood remained despondent much like the low clouds overhead.

No matter how many times I told her that at least it would not be as cold when we got to Durban. She wanted the sun and to feel its warmth. She said she didn't come all this way to have the same weather which was the norm most days in the UK.

I suggested if she didn't believe it would get better, she should keep an eye on the temperature reading, and by the time we got to Kit's house it was 18c, almost double the day before. Yes it might still be drizzle and rain, but at least warmer.

I had not seen Kit for over 15 years, and when we got to the house, there was another surprise waiting for me.

My other brother Nick had flown down from Cape Town for the night.

The 3 brothers reunited after almost 2 decades!!

After all the introductions, we all had a couple of hours before Kit and Nina had to leave and open their restaurant called Kung Thai.

The house or to be more accurate the boardinghouse reminded us both of a railway station with residents and their friends coming and going at all times, and by the looks of it all were welcome to spend the night if need be.

What gave Helen and I even more pleasure was the amount of dogs.

Let me start with the dogs from big to small, then introduce you to the people.

The biggest dog by far was tau, a Rhodesian ridgeback, and as with most big dogs, not much personality.

Next came Gizzie, a jack rustle, full of personality, followed by Mini another jack rustle, with equal amounts of personality, and finally Boss the most recent resident.

With our 4-legged friends accounted for, let me In no particular order introduce you to Kim, in her 40s, a freelance photographer and owner of boss, followed by Glen also in his 40s IT specialist, and x army and owner of Mini. The final adoptive dog owner is Chris late 30s, also an IT specialist and owner of Gizzie.

Gizzie was abandoned at the house by a previous tenant, and kit took him under his wing.

Now with the dogs and their owners taken care of, 2 other residents remain.

Theresa or T as she is known in her mid 30s a teacher, and finally Chrissie also mid 30s, an employee at one of the local museums.

Poor Helen, it was not only my brother Kit and his girlfriend she had to meet, but also Nick as well as all the others from the "digs".

It soon became apparent that the dogs were quite used to people coming and going, and I don't just mean the residents, but their friends and friends of friends.

As you can imagine when 3 members of the same family let alone brothers get together, there is quite a lot of tomfoolery, and there certainly was that night.

Helen spent most of the night with a bemused expression on her face, no doubt wondering what she had let her self in for. 3 brothers in their late 50s and early 60s, behaving like teenagers.

Was this what she had traveled almost 10,000 kilometres to witness and experience?

While I can't speak for Helen, I think a good time was had by one and all.

Day 4

I had better tell you about Durban, before continuing with my story.

Little is known about the first residents, hunter gatherers. The first European settlers arrived in the area later to be called Durban in 1824 and were met by the then Zulu king Shaka.

One of the settlers was a man called Fynn, who helped the king to recover from a serious battle stab wound. To show his gratitude king Shaka handed over a strip of land about 50 kilometres by 160 kilometres to the British settlers.

The British set up a sugar cane industry in the 1860s. Farmers had a difficult time getting Zulu labourers to work on their plantations, so the British brought thousands of bonded labourers from India on twenty five-year contracts to work in the sugar plantations.

As a result of the importation of Indian labourers, Durban has the largest Asian community on the African continent, and the largest Indian population outside of India.

Today, Durban is the busiest container port in Africa and a popular tourist destination with its almost all year round subtropical climate.

One of the features of this seaside city is its so-called

Golden mile of white sandy beaches. It became known as the holiday capital of the country, with Johannesburg its nearest major city.

The province is also not that far from Swaziland and Mozambique.

Another feature for me is the great curry served at almost all restaurants, cafes, takeaways, and even street food vendors.

History lesson over with, let's return to the present.

Kit's garden is surrounded by many indigenous trees and shrubs. Ideal for the Hadeda, and early each morning, the bird could be heard outside our bedroom window.

It didn't take us long to fall in love with Gizzie and Mini, and we would have gladly kidnapped them and brought them back to Wales with us.

Before going to bed the previous night, we took Gizzie and Mini to bed with us and when we woke up the next morning, found Gizzie tucked up and fast asleep inside one of the open suitcases.

During our stay with Kit, the 2 dogs would sleep in our bedroom each night. One would either be on the bed or in a chair, or in the suitcase.

Every time we sat outside on the pool patio, the 2 dogs would jump on the bench next to us.

Gizzie is probably one of the most talkative dogs I have ever known.

The more you stroked him, the more he issued grunts

of pleasure, and the closer he would try and get to you.

One of the many plans on the to do list today would be a guided coach tour of Durban. I hasten to add, that I was not the guide.

We had to be at the departure point by 9am, and having set off in time we made our way to the CBD.

The bad weather continued along with our bad luck.

By the time we reached what we thought was the departure point, we discovered, the satnav had taken us to the wrong building.

In the rain, we were pointed in several directions, but all proved to be wrong.

Finally having given up any idea of a coach tour, we found our way back to collect our car in the secure car park, when another obstacle was put in our way.

The pay machine only took small denominations, and all we had was R100 notes.

A black couple standing next to us, who overheard our problem stepped forward, and kindly offered to pay for us.

This goodwill gesture, though small, meant a lot to both of us, and even months later, Helen can't forget their generosity.

Wet and dejected, we drove back to the house or as it was called, the "digs".

When we got back, there was at least one bit of good news. My credit cards had arrived.

Kit decided it was time to introduce Helen to a proper

Durban currey that lunchtime.

Durban currey here we come!! The 3 of us went to one of kit's favourite currey dens.

If you read about our previous curry experience in Cape Town, you will know that I love Cape Malay Kerrie as well as Durban curry.

Of course the chicken and mutton currey once again came with bones in them, so Helen settled on the beef. She also got to try curried trotters but judging on her facial expression was evidently not taken with this delicacy.

Kit offered her a bit more, but she politely declined the offer, and returned to her beef curry.

After dropping Kit back at his house, it didn't take Helen long to inform me, that she also didn't like the taste of Durban curry either.

That afternoon we made our way to Gateway shopping centre, or as it is called "Gateway Theatre of shopping".

The mall is built on an old sugar plantation, and has 18 movie theatres, 6 Nouveau Cinemas, a playhouse called the Barnyard Theatre, more than seventy restaurants, more than 350 stores, the Wave House, an arcade and theme park called Fantasy Forest, a skate park, the highest indoor climbing rock in the world, the highest fountain in Africa, a gym, tenpin bowling, dodgem cars, valet parking,a Gallery, Palm Court, 1 on 1 adventure golf, a science centre and theme park, and a 4x4 track.

We managed to do a bit of window shopping, before

going to watch a musical tribute show at the Barnyard theatre in the mall.

The theatre was much like a bistro. However, patrons were allowed to take in their own food if they wanted, but had to buy any drinks from the theatre.

Fortunately for us, there was a branch of Panarottis near by. While she had a pizza, I had one of the pasta dishes.

Helen seemed to enjoy the show even though it was very South African in its humor. She certainly enjoyed watching many of the other people that night letting their hair down.

Day 5

We woke up once again to the sound of the Hadeda and believe it or not something bright in the morning sky; it was the sun!!!

A relaxing morning was spent at the "digs" before returning to Gateway shopping mall to investigate what it had to offer.

The previous afternoon we had very little time to walk through the Mall, mainly due to my hip problem.

That evening we went to an old favourite in Durban called the Stables, a night time market.

It is housed in the old New Market Stables in Durban, which were previously used as stables for horses. The market consists of about 230 stables, each one having been converted in to a little shop or business.

Once upon a time the main focus was on arts and crafts combined with the unique and the unusual.

It still has the look and feel of stables each named after famous race horses in which the stalls are situated.

Visitors can find a wide and interesting variety of goods including clothing, antiques, books, toys, make-up, paintings, embroidery and cell phone accessories. The market also includes several food stalls and a pub.

Years before, I had visited the market several times but during the passing years, as with so many things in South Africa; it had deteriorated.

The market today is dominated with cheap goods from China and very little home grown items, but there were still some nice Indian food stalls.

After about one and a half hours at the market, we made our way to Kit's restaurant and spent the rest of the night there, until it was time to go home.

Day 6

It was an early call today. Kit and 2 of his friends and I were going to go out on his boat for a couple of hour's early morning fishing.

By 6am we were heading out to sea to look for our first catch. Helen had decided to stay at home, and catch up with some sleep.

The 4 of us caught a few fish, bringing the bigger catch back with us, which would be cooked by Nina later.

While many fishermen tell of the big one that got away, I was fortunate that day to have landed the biggest fish.

As you can imagine, I didn't let Kit forget it, and suggested I buy him some fishing lessons for his next birthday.

In the afternoon we were going on a game drive at Shongweni Game reserve, about 30 kilometres outside Durban.

Before it was time to drive to the game reserve, kit, Nina and the residents had told us about a really good Saturday morning market.

Let the owners of the Essenwood Craft Market tell you them selves.

"It is situated in a near by park under a lush canopy of evergreen trees, and is focused on the entire family. The kiddies play area is conveniently situated right next to our Food Court enabling parents to keep a close eye on their children at play while they enjoy a meal or 'cuppa' in a lively and sociable atmosphere complimented by the music of one of our many buskers."

The variety of food was extremely good ranging from organic breads and products to curreys, traditional South African, Italian, Greek and so much more.

The stalls situated on either side of the foot paths were also very good with a wide variety of hand made crafts, and other goods.

The market and the sun had certainly helped Helen's mood and she was now finally happy to be back in South Africa.

This market was far better then the Stables. There was not much if any Chinese junk for sale.

Our tummies full and having enjoyed some lovely coffee, we made our way to the beech front.

Another tourist site from the past was Mini Town on the beachfront.

Mini town was established more than thirty years ago on Durban's Golden Mile. The buildings are scaled down to 1:24 of their size. The buildings reach just above knee height.

Apart from the well known city buildings, the miniature trains and planes move around the train station and airport. There is even a miniature harbour with ships.

I wanted to see if this too had been neglected or not. I also thought Helen might enjoy wondering around it.

After Mini Town, we went to the beachfront market, which was very poor.

Typical African craft aimed at tourists, and not very original. I guess if you are an overseas tourist you would be happy with their offerings.

While the weather had improved, our ongoing bad luck was set to continue.

When we reached the game reserve, we were told because of the amount of rain in the past few weeks, the manager didn't know if we would be able to go out on a game drive.

He said he would ask the ranger to take us, but couldn't guarantee how far we would get.

Things were looking up when the ranger arrived, but our optimism was short lived.

The driver come game ranger did not speak much English, and apart from pointing out "there's a buck" and that's a "bird", he didn't know what they were called.

The 3 hour game drive was to say the least a waste of time, with not many animals and birds to see, and even if there were, we would not have known what they were.

Helen said on our way back to Durban she enjoyed the drive in the 4x4, but as for game, what game?

During our breakfast chats with the couple we had earlier met in Howick; Stuart and Rieva, they had recommended what they thought was the best steak house in the country.

This was a recommendation we couldn't miss out on,

and when visiting Joops, we were not disappointed. They were right!! It must be the best steak house in the country if not the continent.

An incident happened that night which really impressed me. Seconds after my rare steak arrived at the table, Joop's wife came to the table and said Joop had asked for the steak to be returned. He said it was not cooked to his high standard, and would probably not be quite to my liking.

Months and even years later, Helen raves about the steak. In fact, on our next trip to Durban, forget about any tourist attractions, this was one of the must places to visit.

Day 7

Once again we woke up to the calls of Hadedas, and after playing with the dogs, it was time to enjoy the sun and warmer weather.

I had planned a visit to show Helen the botanical gardens, but with my hip playing up and now living on pain killers, I didn't know how far I would be able to walk that day.

These gardens include a herbarium, an orchid house, a Cycad collection, a garden for the blind and a charity tea garden.

Even though there were benches scattered through out the site, I still found it difficult and painful to walk to the next bench.

I felt extremely sorry for Helen, knowing that she would have liked to have seen more, but my hip wouldn't allow it.

We or rather I struggled on until we got to the tea garden.

Having ordered tea, coffee and a couple of cakes we sat down under one of the many trees to enjoy the tranquility and the open space.

While we were enjoying our tea and coffee, we were joined by a friendly cat.

He let us stroke him, and remained with us until it was time to leave.

Before leaving the digs that morning, we had arranged with Kit to meet him down at the Durban Undersea Club or (DUC) as it is known by locals.

The (DUC) is a family orientated, social activities club for people that have an interest in the ocean and its beaches. Scuba Diving, Spear fishing, Underwater Hockey, Underwater Photography, Boating, Surf Ski, and Marine Aquarist are some of the leisure activities offered at the club.

It even has a fully equipped dive locker with a 450lt/min air and nitrox compressor and 12 sets of SCUBA Equipment for hire.

The beach at the (DUC) is between Ushaka Marine World and the northern harbour breakwater.

When we arrived at the DUC, we had to be signed in by Kit or any member of the club.

We first walked down to the waters edge, and when we returned to the club discovered to our surprise that most of the residents from the Digs were there as well.

The setting is lovely with tables on the lawns in front of the club house.

It seemed like a favourite gathering place not only for the Digs community, but other people wishing to enjoy a Sunday afternoon drink.

The club has erected a 24-7 webcam for those interested in seeing what is going on day and night.

We enjoyed a relaxing time down at the beach before it was time to head back to the Digs.

Every Sunday evening Kit and Nina invited the residents to a barbecue or roast, and tonight was no exception. All the residents would attend, not to mention any of their friends and even friends of friends, and this would prove to be the case which we discovered later that evening.

Day 8

It was our penultimate day in Durban and we had planned to spend most of it at Ushaka Marine World.

The venue included: a water park named Wet and Wild; with several rides, an aquarium named Sea World; a beach; several restaurants; modeled on boats, and an open air shopping mall; with a host of unique outdoor adventure surf and ethnic clothing shops, and a variety of curio stores.

We wanted to spend the morning at Wet and Wild going up and down on all the slides, after which Helen was going to do a shark cage dive.

I had previously told Helen it would be better and quieter if we went to Ushaka Marine World on a Monday.

Well, our bad luck was set to continue that day.

When we got there, we discovered Wet and wild was closed every Monday, and also that the shark cage dive only took place later in the week.

This misadventure was my fault. I had not bothered to check on opening times before we left for our holiday.

Oh well, back to some last minute shopping.

That evening we took Kit, Nina and one of the residents Kim out for a Portuguese meal.

While we all were enjoying our various perri perri dishes, Kit suggested that if we visited him again, he and

Nina would take some time off from their restaurant and take us to a game reserve in Northern Natal for a few days.

Before even consulting Helen, I said that would be a deal, and we would definitely be back again next year.

Secretly I thought to my self, this offer would save me having to find another reason to visit Durban. Helen's experience of Durban and KZN had not been the best, and I felt sure if she was offered the choice, would not want to return to this province.

Day 9

Our final morning in Durban, and it was time to say goodbye to not only our new 4-legged friends, but also all those at the "digs".

The 250 kilometre drive would take us to Bergville in the northern drakensberg for a few nights.

This time instead of driving along the N3, we would turn off at the Winterton off-ramp and make our way via the back roads to Bergville for the last 3 nights.

Driving via Winterton to Bergville would mean Helen would be able to see much more of the berg and its surrounds.

On our way to the guest house, we visited various craft shops, and stopped to have lunch at a picturesque restaurant.

Late that afternoon we arrived and met the owner Chantal, who showed us to our cottage.

The cottage one of 7 is situated on a 1650 acre estate, with mountain views of the Northern and Central Drakensberg, including the Maluti Mountains and peaks of the so-called the little Drakensberg.

With in minutes of unpacking the car, another 4-legged creature arrived, who would become yet another friend.

Butch served as policeman and warden. Apparently he would inspect each new arrival, and would be round the next day to make sure everything was in order.

He appeared each day as soon as we opened the door, walk in, and lie down on the carpet completely relaxed and watching us.

That night we made do with a selection of cold meat, cheese from the area and some of the nicest avocados we were luckily enough to buy from a roadside seller.

Day 10

While sitting outside on the veranda listening to the birds, including the hadeda, we enjoyed a leisurely breakfast of croissants, homemade butter and jams, while making plans to explore the drakensberg.

My to do list did not include the last few days; there was no hurry to be anywhere.

We would simply drive around while Helen took in the sites of the Drakensberg.

Later that Morning, we made our way through the uKhahlamba Drakensberg Park, a combined Cultural and Natural World Heritage Site until we got to Cathedral Peak hotel.

After walking across manicured lawns, we went into the hotel to have a look around, but were disappointed in the hotel shop.

It was time for a cup of coffee and snack, so we went and sat outside looking over the lawns at the distant mountains.

That night we decided to have a barbecue and relax in the cool evening air.

Butch joined us, and I am not sure if he too enjoyed the cool evening air, or just the pieces of meat we gave him to eat.

While sitting out on the veranda, Helen saw a

shooting star, the first she had seen during all our visits to the country.

Day 11

The day began with another leisurely breakfast on the veranda with some of the left overs from the previous night's barbecue. Butch joined us as he made himself comfortable on the carpet keeping a watchful eye on us.

This was our penultimate day in the country and we would spend it driving around taking in the scenery.

For once there was no need to hurry from place to place. It didn't matter if we took the wrong road or not.

Many years before when I lived in Natal, my band and I performed at most of the resorts in the southern and northern Drakensberg.

The day was very much like traveling down memory lane as we drove past several of the long forgotten hotels and resorts.

In the evening after the trip down memory lane, we went and had a meal at Bingelela, one of the very few restaurants in Bergville.

After the endless grassland of the berg, it made a change to find a different setting.

A thatched area held up by carved tree trunks overlooks the bar and swimming pool.

We first ordered something to drink from the bar, before taking a seat at one of the tables under the thatch.

Bingelela is one of these restaurants which seemed to offer a bit of everything or something for everyone. This invariably means that all the food is average without ever being outstanding.

After making her way through the wide selection of food from curry, to seafood, steaks, pizza, Mediterranean and South African, Helen ordered the gorgonzola rump with melted Roquefort, while I tried their Natal curry.

I was surprised that in this backwater, both meals were well presented and extremely appetizing.

My only criticism was the owners or manager appeared not to pay any person of colour the same amount of attention or respect.

I would have thought after more than a decade, people had got used to an equal society. Mind you, I guess old habits die hard for some.

Day 12

The end of the holiday had arrived, and it was time to make our way back the 350 kilometres to Johannesburg.

Before heading to the airport, we went to Pretoria to visit my son Jade, who I had not seen since he turned 16.

The meeting was mainly due to Helen's insistence.

We got to his house at about 5pm and were introduced to his wife and 2 young children Davin 3 years old and Layla 18 months and their 2 rottweilers.

Jade and his wife Nina suggested that we all go out to a near by restaurant for a quick meal before we had to drive back to the airport; hand back the car, and make our way to the international departure terminal, to board the plane just before midnight.

Driving back to the airport after the meal, Helen did witness a passing highveld thunderstorm. I had often told her about these thunderstorms, but until a person actually experiences this, words will never convey the true sensation.

Day 13

About 7 hours later after taking off from Johannesburg, we landed in Dubai. The temperature outside that morning was a cool 32c.

We had booked a one night stay in one of the cities hotels, and decided to get a taxi to the hotel to see if we could get an early check in.

The hotel terms and conditions stated guests could only check in after 10am and it was only 8am. It was also Friday and know doubt; most Muslim shops are closed on Friday until after dark.

Fortunately, the receptionist found a room for us, and after a shower, we were able to sleep for a couple of hours.

When we walked out of the hotel shortly before lunchtime the temperature had risen to 42c.

Thankfully we soon discovered that every taxi and all public transport have air conditioning, as we made our way by road to the Dubai creek to board a motorized dhow to take us on a tour of the creek.

Needless to say, even with the breeze of the water, it still remained incredibly hot, and unlike Helen, I couldn't wait to get back on to dry land and to get into any building or vehicle which had air conditioning.

After disembarking, we made our way through one of

the many souks, with traders pestering us with offers at every step.

Once we had finished walking through the souk, we went to the Dubai Mall, and at last cool air.

The aquarium on the ground floor in the mall boasts one of the largest tanks in the world, with its 33,000 living animals, including 400 sharks and rays.

I think the motto for this city should have been "we can make everything better, bigger and brighter than any where else".

One of the things which struck me, and which I have not seen or rather smelt in any other mall, was the constant smell of floral fragrance being pumped through the entire building. It was not overpowering, but subtle and pleasant.

We also got to see the Burj Khalifa, the tallest building in the world, but did not want to wait in a 2 hour line to go up to the observation platform.

In the evening while still at the mall we went to one of the numerous restaurants to have a meal and to wait for the musical fountain to light up the skies.

The over 6 thousand coloured lights light up the jets of water as it is sent 500 feet into the air.

The musical fountain was in a way a big disappointment. The fountain only comes to life every 30 minutes or so and the spectacle only lasts about 5 minutes.

After the meal and musical fountain, we got a taxie

back to the hotel at about 9pm and decided to go for a swim on the roof top pool.

Even at that hour, the temperature gauge in the water registered 32c.

We had a couple of hours sleep before it was time to return to the airport, to catch our flight back to London.

While Dubai is impressive, it is a place without soul or heart.

I am glad we stopped over, but not a place I would want to return to.

Our next trip to South Africa had already been decided. We had to be back in Durban in March the following year.

Kit was the ideal person to go on a game drive with. He had previously spent a couple of years in the bush, and was a regular visitor to the game reserve.

I wanted Helen to have a true game reserve experience, and hopefully to see the big 5 in a natural environment.

While the weather, my hip and the timing to visit some of the shops and venues had been wrong, I still enjoyed our latest visit. However, I did feel sorry for Helen. It had not been a great time for her.

I secretly promised my self, I would make it up to her on our next trip.

Journey 4

Fishing for hyenas

This time our latest trip to South Africa started at Birmingham International airport, and take us via Schiphol airport Amsterdam on the outward bound flight and via Charles De gaulle Paris on the return trip.

The decision to fly these routes was based on purely selfish reasons.

I wanted to fly on the A380, and Air France was the only airline operating this plane into South Africa.

During one of our previous visits I mentioned I was an aviation journalist for a while, but even if I was not, I am still a geek when it comes to flying on different aircraft.

There are those, who love trains, or even cars, but for me it has always been planes, and for obvious reasons not plain spotting.

Many years ago on a trip to London, I was able to make 5 stop overs before reaching Heathrow. At the time when planning and booking my flights, I made sure I departed from each city on a different aircraft. This was in the days, when SAA only used Boeing aircraft; an opportunity to travel in other makes of aircraft.

To date, I have flown on a 707, 727, 737, 747, 757, 767, 777, including variants of these aircraft, and as I write this, next want to fly on the 787.

When it comes to Airbus, I have flown on the following aircraft. The A300, A310, A318, A319, A320, A321, A330, A340, and shortly it would be the A380.

While on the subject of European aircraft, I was lucky to have also flown on Concorde.

This trip to South Africa meant we departed at 6am from Birmingham, fly to Amsterdam, and land in Johannesburg later that night.

It was Helen's first day time flight. I much prefer doing the trip this way, even though you could argue I have missed out on a day, but found I don't feel as tired after arriving at the final destination.

Day 1

The flight that day was uneventful, apart from a surprise when the KLM cabin crew offered me their safety pamphlet in Braille. This was the first and only time during all my travels any airline has carried Braille instructions on board.

Before Helen began watching movie after movie, she said "let's hope this trip will be better than the last trip, or shall I call it a pilgrimage?"

On arrival at about 11pm in Johannesburg, my son Jade was there to meet us, and we went back to his house.

When biltong, dry wors and brandy and coke appeared while we sat outside on the patio, I knew we were back in South Africa. The only other thing to make our visit complete would be the call of the Hadeda, but I would have to wait until the next morning to hear the call.

I don't know if the 2 dogs remembered us, or it might be the smell of biltong, but it didn't take them long to arrive and sit with us.

Shortly after the biltong appeared, Jade came out with a couple of packets of koeksisters; a surprise for Helen, and she too knew she was back in the country.

Jade's wife Nina was away in Cape Town on business

and their 2 kids were with her parents for the night.

After much chat, much biltong, several koeksisters and several brandy and cokes, it was time for bed.

Day 2

Our to do list started today with a trip to Tan' Malie se Winkel near the Hartbeespoort dam, where we would enjoy our first barbecue of the holiday.

This shop used to be a favourite of mine when I worked in Johannesburg, and would often go there with friends on a Sunday, the only day it is open.

A Good nights sleep meant Helen and I felt rested after our flight the day before.

We had to wait for Nina's parents to drop off Davin and Layla before we could set off to find Tant Malie.

Traveling from Pretoria to the shop, The 2 kids spent the next hour crying for their "mommie."

The crying only stopped if Helen distracted them, and the same applied when we were having our barbecue.

It wouldn't have been that bad, if they were real tears, but they were crocodile tears.

We later discovered that if Nina was there on her own with the kids, they would then begin crying for their "daddy".

It took a lot of self control not to say anything, especially as I didn't think it was fair to expect Helen, who after all was on holiday to look after the kids.

Before I say too much, let me tell you about Tan' Malie se Winkel.

The building reminds one of an old time country trading post dating back to the previous century with its tin roof, fronted by a lace-edged veranda.

Once you have chosen your barbecue spot under one of the trees, a member of staff arrives pushing a wheel barrow full of hot coals, and pours them into the barbecue.

The glowing coals now in their place, it was time to head back to the veranda, and choose from a selection of meat. After the platter of meat has been weighed there is a selection of salads and sauces and not forgetting pap, a polenta or maize porridge to choose from.

If you still have room after the meal, there is always coffee and milktart and other puddings.

Before leaving, we went to have a look at the shop which sells some novelty products ranging from pottery, handcrafts, home made jams and preserves.

What should have been a pleasurable outing was quite honesty a stressful trip and hardly an enjoyable meal.

We got back to Jade's house later that afternoon, and thankfully Nina, the mother of these 2 demanding kids arrived back from Cape Town at about 7pm.

Once the kids were in bed, we chatted for a while, before it was time for bed.

Tomorrow would be a busy day. Jade was first going to drop us off at one of the Gautrain stations, to catch the gautrain; South Africa's first and only high speed rail link. The train would take us back to the airport to pick up our car.

We intended starting the day with some shopping, then visit the Cullinan diamond mine, then stop to have a look at the Union buildings.

Day 3

After some trouble purchasing our train tickets, we walked on to the platform to wait for the train which runs between Pretoria and Johannesburg.

The train was spotless, on time, and extremely quiet. I wonder how long it will remain like this?

When we got to the airport we first found a cell shop to buy some air time before making our way to collect the car.

I had forgotten that any transaction in Africa always takes longer than any where else in the world; part of so-called "African time."

By the time we had the keys in our hand we were running late, and it was time to find a restaurant.

We decided to go to Moo Moo Wine Bar, a steak house, which offered traditional cuisine.

We had not had breakfast before leaving, and by the time we got to the restaurant we were both ravenous.

"How nice to be out of the household" I said to Helen as we sat down to look at the menu.

"What do you mean?"

"Well Penguin, on Sunday, I had to bite my lip not to say anything."

"Why?"

"It was not fair on you. You are on holiday and you are

certainly not a nurse maid."

"I didn't mind."

"I know, but it was not your duty to look after those kids. Anyway Penguin, let's forget them, what do you fancy on the menu?"

We both decided to try the mango and biltong salad while Helen had a skewer of chicken wings, red peppers with garlic and a perri perri dressing and shoestring fries, while I had a perri perri steak.

As it was almost lunch time, and way past breakfast desert seemed a good idea.

Helen had a white chocolate and cranberry spring roll topped with vanilla ice cream, while I ordered a rum and raisin ice cream desert, which turned out to be one of its kind. The flaming rum and raisin as it is called arrives at the table with flames enveloping the ice cream. The ice cream unlike many restaurants which serve this dish was in this case not the main item on the plate.

The rum and the huge raisins which had been soaked in liquor for a week stole the show.

Even when the alcohol had been burnt off, the flames from the raisins continued to burn for minutes after the dish arrived at the table.

There was also something else different about this restaurant; it sold old-time jams, which you certainly do not see in any supermarket. The waitress even brought us some of the jams and preserves to sample.

After the meal, we did a bit of shopping.

"Why hurry, we are on holiday." I said to Helen as we went from shop to shop.

By the time we got to cullinan, we had missed our appointment.

"We'll have to go back next time" I told Helen, but there was no reply as we drove back towards Pretoria.

Our next stop would be the Union buildings.

These buildings were erected on a disused quarry and were completed in 1913, and at a height of 60 metres inhabit the highest point in the city and are surrounded by large terraced gardens.

They form the official seat of the South African government and also house the offices of the president of the country. The building and garden is also one of many South African heritage sites.

The matching statues on top of the domed towers are Atlas, holding up the world, and the statue on the domed rostrum in the amphitheatre between the wings is Mercury, a mythic Roman messenger and a god of trade, while the clock chimes are identical to those of Big Ben in London.

This is where Mandela was inaugurated as the first democratically elected president of South Africa.

When we got to the Union buildings, we parked the car and walked down the street to allow Helen to get a better look at this iconic building.

"It certainly looks impressive, or at least the bit I can see" said Helen as we stood on the pavement.

I could not believe how many street sellers and vagrants had taken up residence on the streets outside the building.

I wouldn't have objected, but the goods for sale were cheap and nasty, all imports from china, which had no association with the building, let alone South Africa.

What a pity, but I guess this is part of the "new South Africa".

Before returning to Jade, we went to one of the shopping malls. I had ordered a couple of books, and needed to collect them.

That night we had another barbecue, and thankfully Nina was there to look after her kids.

Even though we had not seen much, it had been a relaxing day.

We didn't stay up too late. We wanted to be on our way early the next morning.

Tomorrow we would be traveling the 160 kilometres to Parys to spend the day and that night with Shirley, a former newspaper colleague of mine.

Day 4

Parys is a little country town on the southern banks of the Vaal River about one hour' from Johannesburg. It is situated within the Vredefort Dome Area the place of the oldest and largest meteorite impact site in the world and was recently declared South Africa's 7th World Heritage Site.

The town was formerly a farming community with the main products being; tobacco, corn, sorghum and cattle. However, in the past few years, many people have built retirement homes in the area, and one of its newest residents was Shirley.

As Shirley warned us, Parys in many ways is a throw back to the past. The town is scattered with art, antique and secondhand shops.

Shirley recently celebrated her 80th birthday, but was still extremely sprightly for her age, and would have put those 20 years younger than her to shame.

I had not seen Shirley for 15 years, so there was a lot of catching up to do.

We arrived at about lunchtime, and after introductions, the three of us and her 2 dogs sat outside on her veranda overlooking the Vaal River. Helen immediately took to Shirley and it goes without saying, the 2 dogs slept, while the 2 women sat chatting and enjoying a cup of coffee.

Unfortunately that afternoon we couldn't spend too much time relaxing and chatting. I had booked a quad bike game drive, and the nature reserve was about 30 kilometers away.

When we arrived at the game reserve, I settled down at the outside bar while Helen and her guide each disappeared on their quad bikes.

About 2 hours later Helen and the guide returned.

She couldn't wait to tell me about her adventure.

How without making too much noise, they hurriedly had to make their way between 3 rhinos, how they came across a giraffe struck dead by lightning, how at close quarters they saw ostrich, impala, zebra, wildebeest, and also a red hartebeest.

"It was fantastic!!"

"Weren't you scared Penguin?"

"Yes, I was, but my guide just said, I had to be quiet, and make sure I went past the rhinos as quick as possible.

It was also amazing to see that giraffe, and to get so close to the other animals."

"What about the bike ride?"

"That was also great. We didn't have to stick to the roads."

It would be an understatement to say Helen really enjoyed her self that late afternoon. If a person could ever resemble Champaign bubbles in a glass, well that was Helen that afternoon.

Arriving back at Shirley's house the plans for the

evening meal had changed. It was a Tuesday, and most of the town's restaurants were closed.

Instead of eating out, Shirley had decided to cook a meal, and invite 2 friends around to join us for dinner.

At midnight we were still all sitting outside and chatting, but her friends had to go, and we needed to get to bed ready for an early start and long drive the next morning.

Day 5

The early start was not to be. Shirley's hospitality knew no bounds.

She insisted on cooking a full English breakfast, and then showing us round the town.

Fortunately for us, there were not too many shops to visit, and we finally said our goodbyes at about lunch time, but not before Shirley gave me a packet of home made hertzog cookies.

Our next destination was Clarens, about 400 kilometres away.

During our previous 3 visits we had become use to the numerous road works and the 10 or 20 minute stop signs. We were certainly not disappointed that afternoon.

The only interesting thing to occur that afternoon was a Free State thunder storm. There was not much rain, but more than enough lightning, judging on the amount of sudden gasps I heard coming from Helen as the bolts of lightning struck the surrounding fields.

A journey which would most days take about 4 hours took us almost 6hours thanks to the number of road works.

Finally we arrived in Clarens as the sun was setting, and we still had to find our castle for the night.

Clarens is known as the jewel of the Eastern Free State.

The village is in the foothills of the Maluti Mountains close to the Golden Gate National Park, and the mountain kingdom of Lesotho.

For years Artists have taken up residence in the town every spring. The number of art galleries and craft shops around the town square is proof of this.

Willows, fruit trees and lombard poplars are found all round the town.

Believe it or not the town has a link in a strange kind of way to the Titanic. In 1912, a former resident noticed a rock formation in the distance which looked much like the titanic, which it has been called since then. The town is also well known for its many fossil sites and rock paintings.

We finally found the road we were looking for; a gravel road which would lead us to our castle for the night.

When we arrived at the gates and after contacting the owner, we were told where to find the keys.

The novelty castle was Helen's choice, so it was only fair to let her be the first one to explore the castle, while I waited in the car.

At the very top, the castle consisted of a bedroom with a 4-poster bed with an en suite bathroom or as they called it Rapunzel's Tower. The next floor down a lounge with an impressive fireplace decked with cherubs in a gold finish, and what the owners claim was a well equipped kitchen and leading off from it

The Chamber of Angels.

This so-called chamber of angels was a 3-sided enclosed shelter with chairs, tables and a barbecue at one end of the patio.

When Helen returned, we took our suitcases inside and after a closer inspection of the castle went back along the gravel road to see what culinary delights the village had to offer.

We decided to try Clementines, a restaurant inside a red and green corrugated iron building, and I don't mean just the roof but all the inside walls were covered with painted corrugated sheeting.

I settled for the Thai beef salad with a sweet chilli and lime dressing followed by their oxtail, while Helen chose the camembert and fig in a phyllo pastry and chicken pot pie, chicken and mushrooms in a creamy white wine sauce.

While the variety of dishes on the menu was exceptional for a small town, the food was average, and unfortunately, the service below average. Not once did the owner Shelly or her staff ask if we were enjoying our meal.

When I pointed this out to her, she seemed not to care. It was obvious; money was the most important thing to her, and not customer satisfaction and service.

During our meal Helen said "I like the idea of sleeping in a fairy tail castle."

"I am glad you like it Penguin, but as you know it

wouldn't have been my choice "

"I wonder what the breakfast will be like tomorrow? I am so glad you pre-ordered it. Mind you, I suppose we could have bought something from one of the shops around here."

Day 6

We woke up to one of the coolest mornings we had experienced since we began our trips to South Africa, but this was hardly surprising considering we were up high in the mountains.

At the requested time our cooked breakfast in 2 treasure chests was delivered to the front gate.

Helen went down the 3 flights of stairs to collect our food, and returned carrying the 2 treasure chests and made her way to the "Chamber of Angels" or as I called it, the patio, where we sat outside and ate our food.

All I can say about the breakfast is it was average. I have certainly tasted better in most places.

After breakfast we packed our bags and put the cases in the car and left to see what the village had to offer.

Always on the look out for any unusual products, we first popped in to The Clarens Village Grocer, then The Purple Onion, and while each had many home made products, there was not much we hadn't seen before.

We then went to one of the coffee shops, which also sold several African grown coffee beans and on request roasted them on the premises to your liking.

Having each ordered a cup of coffee we went and sat

outside. The town or village certainly had that village feel to it, but admittedly this was not the height of the annual artist invasion or holiday season.

We would liked to have visited the local Brewery and perhaps sampled some of the ales and ciders, but it was closed when we got there, and we had a 400 kilometre drive to Durban via the Golden Gate Highlands National Park and winterton.

Looking back, the novelty castle in my opinion is fine for a night, but I can think of many other and better places I would prefer to stay in. I also think some of the claims made in the blurb found on the internet are a bit over the top. A good example of this is the claim that on the patio you will find plush furniture. I would have said basic patio furniture.

The outstanding feature of the Golden Gate Highland national park is the sandstone cliffs, which take on a golden colour when the sun shines on them.

If you are lucky you might also see black wildebeest, eland, blesbok, oribi, springbok, Burchell's zebra and the rare bearded vulture.

On our slow drive through the park we managed to see in the distance a few black wildebeest, blesbok, and oribi, but sadly no vultures.

Once through the park it was on to Winterton and then on to the N3 and down to Durban.

Before we reached Durban and then on to Kit my brother, we first stopped and had lunch at the Pot and

Kettle, the restaurant in the valley of a thousand hills which we had visited on our previous trip, but thanks to the foul weather that time, the views of the countryside were down to about 10 metres.

As we sat outside each enjoying a burger and a slice of home made cheese cake Helen said "This is more like it."

"Are you talking about the food?"

"No, the warm sunshine and views of the distant hills!

I can't believe it is the same place we visited last time."

After lunch we continued our journey with the next planned stop on our to do list at Daniela's Deliciously Decadent in Hillcrest to allow Helen to buy some cookies.

A cup of coffee and a cookie later, we were on our way again, and the final stop would be Kit's restaurant Kung Thai, to pick up the keys to the house and then on to the Digs.

As the electric gates rolled open to the digs, and we drove in, there was much barking from all the dogs, but when we stopped and called them to us, there was much wagging of tails, and believe it or not, not a whiff of biltong.

After first stroking the dogs, then hand shakes and hugs and hellos from the residents, it was time to catch up with all the latest news. We finally left, and went back to Kit's restaurant for a meal.

In a strange kind of way, it seemed if we had only seen everyone the week before, yet it was almost 7 months.

That night as per usual, Gizzie and Mini slept in our room.

Day 7

As if to order, the Hadeda calls woke us up, and after giving the dogs some biltong, we went through to the kitchen and then on to the patio for a cup of coffee. A couple of minutes later, Gizzie and Mini joined us on the bench.

Today we were returning to ushaka Marine World, and hopefully this time get to go on all the rides at Wet and Wild, and Helen to do her shark dive.

We got there pretty early, and yes!! It was open.

I had not been to a water park for probably about 20 years, and it was fun to go on all the rides again.

Helen went on some, but not liking heights, she refused to go on the highest rides.

About 2 hours later, we decided it was time for Helen to meet up with the sharks, or was it the sharks to meet Helen?

I sat outside and waited for her to return, or if things went wrong, for her to return in pieces.

Things went well, and Helen returned about 30 minutes later in one piece. She said it was exciting, and was glad we were finally able to visit the resort.

That night we returned to the Stables night market, and as expected nothing had changed or improved. All the same vendors and the same products were still there.

After the Stables, look out!! Joops and a fillet steak here we come or to give its correct title Joop's Place.

This was the one meal and the one restaurant we had spoken so much about after returning to the UK, and yearned to visit again.

In case you think I am being paid to promote this restaurant, I am going to quote Jennifer Anderson, who dined at the restaurant and posted her comments on the internet."This place was amazing. The appetizers were interesting, the wine list was deep with choices and the Dutch themed interior was cozy and nice. The service was excellent and the star of the evening - the steak. Obviously a labor of love and a product of over 20 years of insistent quality and flavour. Every kind I tried was mouth watering, tender, flavorful, and always an outstanding cut. The peppercorn steak, a specialty, was perfectly cooked without a burnt crust and still wonderfully tender. The sauces are decadant and the sides hearty. This is not something any meat ea

I have to endorse Jennifer, and congratulate her on her good taste and appreciation of the best. If you are ever in Durban, you will have to visit Joop's Place and try the fillet steak.

Now happy and contented, we went back to the digs and after a cup of coffee took the dogs with us to bed.

Day 8

One good thing about living in Durban or visiting the digs: we didn't need an alarm clock. The Hadeda's made sure we were awake at sunrise.

Today would start with a fishing trip, followed by a visit to the market.

Helen decided to join Kit and me down at the beach.

After a quick cup of coffee, it was time to get the bait out of the freezer, rods in the car, and the boat and trailer hitched to the car. The 3 of us were ready to leave for the beach and Kit and I ready to catch that big one.

When we got to the beach, Helen and I were introduced to 2 friends of kit, who would join us at sea.

Launching the boat took some precision timing.

Once the boat and trailer were attached to a 4x4, the boat with pilot on board would be reversed into the oncoming waves and quickly pushed off the trailer, before the 3 of us quickly guided the boat as far out into the water as we could before jumping onboard, and the outboard motor started.

After this had been successfully accomplished, we waved goodbye to Helen, who was sitting on the beach with a cup of coffee reading a book and enjoying the sun rise.

We were on our way to find that big one thanks to the onboard fish finder.

The water was dirty, which meant today would not be a good day for any biggies, and after about 40 minutes, we decided nonetheless to cut the engines and try our luck.

According to the fish finder, there seemed to be a shoal of small fish beneath us. We all decided to use the daisy chain approach, which meant placing several hooks one above the other.

This method worked well, as we all brought in several fish each time.

We moved to a few other places, but the catch remained the same.

Shortly before calling it a day, I managed to hook what felt like quite a big one, and with the others watching, I slowly began to reel it in.

About 2 metres from the boat my fish broke free, and almost instantly a shark which the others agreed must have weighed about 100 kilograms jumped out of the water; no doubt in hot pursuit of my fish.

Quite what would have happened to me if the shark had taken my fish I will never know, but as has happened with many a fisherman, the big one this time got away. I hope the shark enjoyed my fish, even if I didn't manage to do so.

It was time to head back to land, have a shower and head off to the market.

Before this could all take place, we had to get the boat as close to the trailer as possible.

When we were near the Shaw, the pilot changed gear

and at full thrust headed straight for the beach, until the boat grounded in the sand and we all jumped off and tried to haul it up as far up the beach as we could.

The 4x4 with trailer behind it then reversed back until we were able to lift the boat on to it.

Unlike my previous fishing trip, this time all we had to show was a few kilos of various small fish, but never the less, Nina would use them in the restaurant later that night.

Helen said she enjoyed her time on the beach, watching people come and go as they launched their boats.

Back to the digs for a quick shower, and then off to Essenwood market.

The market had not changed since our previous visit some 7 months earlier. It was nice to see the wide selection of food, and to sit out under some trees and watch the morning and people go by.

After meandering through the market and stalls, we made our way to one of the near by shopping centres.

We needed to get some provisions for our trip to the game reserve the next morning.

Shopping almost complete, we called in at a new organic meat supplier to collect some meat to take with us to the game reserve.

Shopping trip completed, it was time to return to the digs to relax.

Later in the afternoon we were joined by Chris. He had recently applied for a new job, and that morning was told he was the successful applicant.

He and T were going to go to a restaurant to celebrate this good news, and they wanted to know if we wanted to join them.

When it came to restaurants, it had to be Joops, and after convincing both of them, even though T was a vegetarian, they agreed we should all meet there that evening.

This was the first time for Chris and t at this gem of a restaurant.

Even though Joop specializes in steaks, T was more than surprised and impressed at her vegetarian platter.

Day 9

Our game safari was about to begin and with it, fishing for hyenas.

Kit had hired a 4x4 and after packing our clothes and collecting our provisions for the next few days, we along with Kit and Nina set out on the 300 kilometre drive to Umfolozi.

The first stop would be Richards Bay for breakfast. Not much was open on a Sunday, but we managed to find a Wimpy.

This fast food outlet was opened in 1967 in Durban, and has for several years run a successful campaign with its offer of an all day breakfast.

The 4 of us enjoyed a hearty breakfast.

Back on the road again, it was about another 100 kilometres before we reached the game reserve and Mpila camp.

When we stopped at the visitor centre to sign in, we were first greeted by a family of inquisitive Warthogs, before driving the 10 kilometers to the self catering Safari Tented Camp at Mpila; our accommodation for the next 2 nights.

Our 2 chalets were about 20 metres apart, and comprised a tented bedroom with en suite shower and toilet and opposite the room across a wooden boardwalk, the kitchen.

Outside both kitchen and bedroom was a veranda, and 1 metre below the raised platform each chalet had its own barbecue facility.

At 10pm each night, the electricity in this unfenced camp was switched off until sunrise the next morning. Fortunately, the oven and fridge in the fully equipped kitchen ran on gas.

A notice in the kitchen told visitors to make sure all doors cupboards and personal items were fully secured and locked to prevent the local troop of monkeys stealing and damaging items.

Within about 10 minutes of making our selves at home, about 5 or 6 chattering monkeys appeared in the near by trees.

It didn't take us long to find out how true the notice was, and what their intention was.

Helen had come out of the bedroom, and forgot to zip up the flap come door to the bedroom. About 2 minutes later while Helen inspected the kitchen, the monkeys saw their chance and scampered into the bedroom.

Turning back to look outside from the kitchen, she saw the last of the monkeys disappearing into our bedroom.

She immediately ran shouting across the boardwalk and chased them out, but not before they had upturned a jar, and stolen some sweets.

As if mocking her, they then sat in the trees eating and dropping the sweets on the ground below.

Another monkey invasion followed later that afternoon,

when she discovered she had left the bathroom window flap open. and when she went in found another intruder in the bathroom.

I think she then realized that monkeys are not such sweet and innocent animals, but more pests.

After a couple of hours relaxing at the camp site, it was time to do an afternoon game drive, and see what we could find during the next 4 hours.

The first animals to be spotted were the plentiful herds of impala, with their reddish coats. During the next 2 days we would see many more either in pairs, or several dozen.

Next we came across some vultures sitting in a tree as we continued our afternoon safari.

Traveling slowly around Umfolozi that afternoon we also saw 3 white rhino in the distance, as well as Blue Wildebeest, Zebra, and 2 giraffe near the road minding their own business, while they looked in the higher branches for something to munch on.

We also saw some Eland, some Kudu, as well as nyala.

Even though Nina in the front passenger seat would look out for anything interesting to the left, and Helen in the back seat would keep on the look out for anything on the right, it would invariably be Kit the driver, who would first spot any animal or bird.

"Stop stop" Helen and Nina said. "I think there's an elephant over there."

Kit stopped and asked "Where do you see it?"

"Over there" the two game spotters pointed.

Kit picked up his binoculars and looking in the direction his passengers had pointed said "That ladies is a rock. I don't think I will be hiring you as elephant trackers."

After returning to the camp, it was time to get ready for a barbecue. We had agreed it should be held at Kits' place.

At about 7pm, Helen and I made our way to their chalet to enjoy our barbecue under African skies in the reserve.

With drinks in hand, we all sat on the veranda waiting for the fire to take and the coals to settle.

It was already dark, when Kit and I decided that Nina and Helen would be in charge of cooking.

Before long the sound of hyenas could be heard in the vicinity. This would be Helen's first true close encounter with wild animals in Africa.

The closer the sound of the hyenas got, the more nervous Helen became.

The hyena is an opportunist and a scavenger, and like most wild animals is weary of humans.

We settled down to steak, lamb chops and of course some boerewors along with 3 different salads Nina had prepared.

After our meal it was time to do some fishing for hyenas according to kit.

He tied a couple of lamb chops to a nylon rope and threw it as far as he could in to the surrounding darkness.

Passing me the other end of the rope, he suggested I tie it around my wrist and wait to see what happened.

I don't know why, but I decided it would not be a good idea to tie the rope around my wrist, and instead wound it loosely around my hand and waited to see what would happen.

Without warning, and in a split second, there was a sound like a small gun being fired as the rope tightened, and at that moment the rope flew out of my hand.

I couldn't believe how quickly and powerful the hit had been, and was more than glad I had not listened to Kit and wound the rope around my wrist. I am sure if I had listened; I would have been sitting with a broken wrist.

With the sounds of hyenas all around us, Helen was some what nervous to walk back to our chalet in the dark, and asked Kit with his torch in hand to accompany us.

While she slept, I could hear Hyenas and other animals of the night close to our tent, but it didn't seem to wake Helen.

Day 10

We were all up by 5am, and with breakfast packed in the cooler box in the back of the 4x4, we left the camp and began our early morning safari.

The first animal we came across was a lion, as it lay resting some 10 metres away from the vehicle. We stopped and waited for about 10 minutes, but it didn't seem in a hurry to move, and was definitely not interested in us.

About half a kilometer further down the road we found a herd of some 12 buffalo grazing next to some trees. Once again, they were only about 10 metres away.

We had been lucky. In less than 24 hours we had seen 3 of the (big 5). The lion, the rhino and the buffalo. Would we get to see the remaining two animals which make up (The big 5) I wondered?

By mid morning we had seen many more of the ever present impala, more Eland, more Kudu, as well as more nyala.

Our journey through the park wasn't only about the bigger animals. We also stopped and watched Redbacked shrike, Fork tailed Drongo, Lilac breasted Roller, and Red billed Woodpecker, Grey Lourie or as it is also known the go-away bird, francolins, Barbets, Plovers and Redbilled woodhoopes to mention just some of the feathered species.

During the morning as we continued our drive, we also saw numerous spiders webs stretched across the road. Helen, who as you know has a fear of spiders couldn't help but gaze in amazement and shudder in disgust at the size of these spiders which she said were the size of her hand.

It must have been about mid morning, when we decided to stop at one of the picnic spots and get out the gas barbecue and begin making our breakfast.

While waiting for Kit and Nina to cook our breakfast, I couldn't help thinking how absurd it was that people could have a picnic in the middle of a game reserve yet were told not to get out of their cars. Did the animals know that picnic areas were for the exclusive use of humans?

Eggs, bacon, boerewors, pork sausages tomatoes and mushrooms were all prepared on the gas barbecue or as it is called in South Africa a skottel braai.

One hour later, we were ready to resume our travels through the park, but by then the sun was high in the sky and getting hotter each minute; the animals would all be resting or seeking a shady place.

We continued our drive for a while, but apart from several impala and some other buck, there wasn't much to see.

Kit suggested we head back to the camp, and relax until it was time to go out again later that afternoon.

Later when we left to resume our search for the remaining

(big 5), we saw 3 rhinos not 5 metres away from our vehicle, as they went about grazing; and Fortunately for us unperturbed by the proximity of the 4x4.

We came across several places and signs where elephants had been during the night. Broken branches were the clue, but unfortunately we did not have any luck trying to find them.

I don't know if it happens at other reserves, but several times passing cars would stop, and tell us what they had witnessed.

Sadly, it was time to return to the camp and start preparing our food for the evening meal.

When we got back, a family of warthogs paid us a visit.

Kit and Nina cooked our meal over the barbecue; once again steak, boerewors and this time lamb Sosaties - kebabs one of Helen's favourites. We ate our meal once again with the sounds of hyenas calling all around us.

Day 11

Our brief safari had sadly come to an end, and time to pack the 4x4, and make our way back to Durban.

We had not seen any elephants, and I said to Helen, if we didn't see any this morning on our way out, we would have to visit the reserve again.

Luck must have been on our side that morning. As we drove towards the reception area, we suddenly came across 3 elephants making their way across the road.

They were in no hurry as they slowly munched their way across the road and in to the bush.

How about that for a stroke of luck I thought? In 2 days Helen had managed to see 4 of the (big 5), so it was only the leopard to go, but he or she would have to wait until we visited the country again.

She had been lucky during our 2 night stay. Many people, who spend days in a game reserve were less fortunate, and hear we were, having seen four of the (big 5).

We stopped at reception to have a look around at the curio shop, but didn't find anything interesting, and certainly not things we could take back with us.

Once back at the digs, Helen and I went shopping that afternoon.

Shopping almost complete, we had to meet Kim, from the digs, a well known Durban photographer. Helen wanted some pictures taken of us down at the beach.

The picture shoot over with, we all made our way to Kit's restaurant.

After returning to the UK on our previous visit, I had kept in touch with Stuart and Rieva, the couple we first met in Howick; and we planned to meet them at Kit's restaurant that night.

When Kim Helen and I got to the restaurant, a surprise awaited all of us.

Unbeknown to Kim, this Stuart guy, who we were going to meet, turned out to be someone she had gone to school with many years before.

I don't know who was more surprised, but it just goes to show at times, what a small world we live in.

I think a good time was had by one and all, but at about midnight, it was time to say our goodbyes, and get back to the digs and to bed.

Next morning it would be back to Johannesburg.

Day 12

After saying goodbye to the dogs, and then to Kit, Nina, Kim, T, Chris and Glen, we began the 570 kilometre journey back along the N3.

Our first stop would be once again the little restaurant at the top of Van Reenen paas, which Helen had grown to love. It seemed every time we traveled on the N3, we would stop off at the restaurant for a coffee, a pot of tea and a bite to eat.

This was Helen's first time to stay in Johannesburg and to drive the streets of the city.

How things have changed? I remember the first time we flew into Johannesburg, and how nervous and apprehensive she was about even leaving the airport, now she was a seasoned visitor and driver.

Driving through Saxonwold, one of the oldest suburbs in the city, Helen couldn't help but notice the Jacaranda trees lining the roads.

When we reached Cotswold gardens guest house we stopped and waited for someone to answer the intercom attached to the electric gate. After announcing our arrival, the gate slowly opened and we drove in.

The owner Janine, was waiting to greet us, and after taking our suitcases to the room, we went outside to the peaceful garden for a quick swim.

During our short stay in Johannesburg, I had planned several places Helen might like to visit. Johannesburg was my old stomping ground. I had worked in the city for more than 20 years.

That evening we went to the Butcher's Grill, which claims to be the best steak house in the country and has apparently won several awards.

Well, who ever voted them the best steak house; either has never been to Joops in Durban nor has not very good taste buds.

Yes, the service was excellent, but as for the steak we each had, it was fine, and probably if we hadn't found Joops would have said it was excellent.

The moral of this part of the story, is never believe all the adverts you hear.

Day 13

Once again the next morning, we awoke to the sound and call of the Hadeda.

After a shower and breakfast, the time had come to give Helen a guided tour around Johannesburg.

It would be a street by street guide. I had worked in the city for more than 20 years, and knew all the streets including one-ways across the city as well as Hill brow off by heart.

As we drove up and down each street, I pointed out where the Rand Daily Mail used to be, where the Star building is, where the Citizen is, and various other landmarks.

After a tour of the CBD, we then made our way past Jubert Park and down past the Citizen Newspaper offices and as far as Ellis Park and then back and up around Hillbrow.

She couldn't believe how derelict and third-world this once city of gold had become.

Some shops windows smashed in, with piles of rubble inside them; others boarded up, and even one stretch of road in Hillbrow was now a sandy patch.

Hillbrow was once a cosmopolitan community, and the first to have gay and lesbian bars; in those days a tourist attraction. Many hotels, nightclubs an even an indoor swimming pool and the country's first 24 hour supermarket could also be found there.

During the 60-70-80s most of the top bands played at various night spots in Hillbrow. It also housed the only record bar where you could buy copies of imported albums. Book shops and even a couple of small theatres made their mark.

I had spent many an evening in various Hillbrow clubs during the 70s and early 80s.

Hillbrow was also a regular gathering place for New Years Eve revelers. However, today on New Years Eve, fridges, tables, beds and chairs are hurled over balconies.

In the 1980s much of the middle class began moving out of the area, which in turn lead to lack of investment, decay of major buildings, and leaving behind an urban slum.

Many years before, Hillbrow claimed to have the highest population density of any area in the country, and this probably remains true to this day. However; unlike the 80s, today the area is populated by many criminals and undesirables from parts of Africa as well as migrants from the townships and rural areas.

Sadly many of the landmarks are also being left to fend for themselves. These include the Great Synagogue in Wolmarans Street between Hillbrow and the Johannesburg CBD, the 270 metre high Hillbrow tower, and the cylindrical shaped 54 storey Ponte City. This residential building was previously one of the city's most sought-after addresses, but with inner-city urban decay, it has become run-down, over-populated, and unsafe.

The only area to receive any attention is the Constitution Hill precinct, on the western edge of Hillbrow; the seat of the Constitutional Court of South Africa.

It left me feeling sad and angry. No different to other parts of Africa, where majority rule was the order of the day and with it, declining standards.

Why is it that once the locals take over, they invariably have to destroy the existing infrastructure?

After the personal guided tour, we made our way back towards the northern suburbs, and on to Montecasino.

First a trip for one hour to the casino, then find some where and something to eat before collecting our tickets for the theatre to watch a comedy.

Helen enjoyed the South African comedy, but her enjoyment was short lived. It was now late at night, and it was the first time to drive in Johannesburg at that hour.

We made it back to the guesthouse without being high jacked or stopped by any bogus police.

Day 14

The call of the Hadeda once again meant it was time to get up. This was our penultimate day in South Africa, and we intended to make the most of the next 36 hours.

Today we were going to The Apartheid museum, and that evening visit the Market theatre to see another Athol fugard production.

After breakfast, I telephoned the theatre to confirm details of our booking.

I was told that the performance that night would not be taking place.

Apparently there was some or other function in front of the Market theatre.

I could not believe what I was hearing. It seemed ludicrous to cancel a performance simply because something was happening outside the theatre.

When I pursued the matter, I was told that canceled performances happened regularly.

Let me tell you a bit about this iconic Johannesburg theatre.

The theatre was founded in Johannesburg in 1976 by the late Mannie Manim and Barney Simon, and was constructed out of Johannesburg's Indian Fruit Market built some 60 years earlier.

It later became known as South Africa's "Theatre of the Struggle".

I doubt if the original owners would be too happy to know that the theatre seemed to cancel performances for the slightest reason. Not even apartheid stopped performances during their time at the Market.

Well, I said to Helen we will just have to find something else to do or to see tonight.

"How about if we have a look at what else is on at the various theatres?

I know, how about going to the Barn yard theatre, I am sure there must be a few in Johannesburg, and you like their set up?"

Even though she didn't say it, I think Helen was secretly glad the Fugard performance had been canceled at the Market. One Fugard performance was more than enough for her.

There were 3 Barn Yard Theatres in and around Johannesburg. The nearest was situated in the Cresta shopping centre, not too far from our guest house.

We phoned the theatre and made a reservation for that night before leaving late that morning for the Apartheid museum.

Visitors walking through the museum would through audio and visual soundtracks get to find out about the rise and fall of apartheid in the country. Film footage, photographs, text panels and artifacts along with human stories showed the events known as apartheid.

After about 2 and a half hours we reached the end. Helen found the experience extremely emotional and moving, but I did think that the museum could have paid tribute to and featured more white people, who also played an important role in bringing down apartheid.

Contrary to what they would want you to believe, it wasn't only theANC, who were responsible for the death of apartheid, even though they continue to twist historical events to suit them selves.

Unfortunately, the "new south Africa" has become very similar to the old South Africa.

National, regional and municipal politicians from the ANC are involved in widespread corruption, nepotism, tender fraud, and theft. The police and prison services have also not changed, with corruption, brutal attacks and killing of innocent people and inmates. The big difference now was the police were killing their own people.

The state broadcaster (SABC) once in the pockets of the previous regime which blatantly slanted news items is now virtually a spokesman for the ANC, and even more one-sided in its reporting.

Before leaving the museum, we had a look at the curio shop, but there was not much on offer. Once again like most of the state or provincial run curio shops most of the items were made in China.

Surely you would have thought these shops would have supported local people.

From the curio shop we made our way to the on site restaurant, and while sitting outside enjoyed a bite to eat.

I don't know where time goes when you are on holiday, but before we knew it, it was early afternoon, and time to drive to the Cresta shopping centre on the other side of the city.

When we got there, and with time to kill, I suggested to Helen we pop in to Milky Lane and have a milk shake and may be even one of their famous waffles.

This chain was opened in 1958 and is also well known for its ice cream birthday cakes.

Helen tried their peanut and honey milk shake while I enjoyed their coffee double thick milk shake.

Having collected our tickets for the tribute musical at the Barnyard theatre, we went on to do some last minute shopping.

The theatre is conveniently situated near several fast food outlets and restaurants. This meant patrons could collect something to eat and take it into the theatre and enjoy their meal while enjoying the show.

Helen wanted a pasta dish, so we went to Panarottis.

While she chose a pizza, I chose one of the many pasta dishes.

After the performance, we made it back to the guest house and got ready for our last night in South Africa.

Day 15

Our last day had sadly arrived, and it would also be the last time on this trip to awake to the sound of the Hadeda.

After breakfast, we packed our bags in the car and made our way to the Saturday Neighbourhood market.

Following the success of The Old Biscuit Mill market in Cape Town, the Johannesburg edition was launched in 2011 in Braamfontein, Johannesburg. The market takes place over two floors, a landmark building featuring a large scale concrete facade by Edoardo Villa. The second floor features an extensive rooftop area with views overlooking the city.

We got there at about 9am, and even then; it was bustling with people as we elbowed our way through the crowds to view each of the stalls.

It would have been nice if we had more time to spend at the market, but we had to drive to Pretoria to see jade and his family.

Jade and Nina had invited us to join them for a late afternoon barbecue before making our way back to the airport.

Where had the time gone? It seemed if we had only arrived the other day, and here we were ready to leave again.

Even though I was sad to leave, at least I had something else on the way back to look forward to.

We would be traveling on the Air France A380, a first for me.

Above African skies, I thought to my self only one more trip to go then my big 5 adventure will be over, but would Helen ever get to see the last member of the (big 5); The leopard?

Journey 5

Looking for a Leopard

This was our fifth trip, and Helen had still not seen a leopard in the wild, which would complete the big 5. Would we find this elusive and nocturnal and secretive animal this time?

Helen had also set her heart on swimming the Midmar mile, and this seemed a good enough reason to visit the country again.

This annual swimming event in KwaZulu-Natal attracts thousands of swimmers each year, who have to swim the mile long event in the Midmar dam within one hour in order to receive a certificate and medal.

Towards the end of our 2 week stay in South Africa this time, I had booked a game drive in the Kruger National park, and this was her last chance to possibly have a leopard encounter, but let's start at the beginning.

Unlike the previous day time trip, we left Birmingham

airport in the evening and arrived at Charles de Gaulle Airport one hour later.

As soon as we entered the terminal, we were told by one of the Air France officials in broken English that our flight to South Africa that night had been cancelled due to "technical reasons".

Using his hands, the official tried to impart the bad news. With each gesture we asked if it was because of snow? Then a tornado? Or a crash that had lead to this delay? Each time he said "yes", while shaking his head.

He pointed us in the direction of the information desk, but all they could tell us and the other passengers it was a "technical fault", but once again the official and other Air France officials could not or would not tell us exactly what the "technical fault" was.

After some confusion and further delays, all the passengers were given a food voucher to use at the airport. This entitled each of us to one sandwich and a cold drink.

Having accepted and eaten the measly offering, we and the other passengers made our way back to the information desk and general mayhem and were told the flight would only be leaving at 2pm the next day.

Three hours later and to be exact, at 12.45am we arrived hungry, thirsty and cold at our hotel.

With 10 minutes to spare before the bar in the hotel closed, we were able to get a hot chocolate to drink before retiring for the night without the prospect of finding some where to eat.

While we had both looked forward to travelling on the A380 again, these pleasurable thoughts had been dashed and were long forgotten thanks to the shoddy service dished out by Air France.

Day 1

The hotel we had been assigned to could only be described as basic. There were no complimentary toiletries and no coffee making facilities provided.

At this stage a stale piece of bread would have been gratefully received, but we were pleasantly surprised the next morning with the choice of food on offer at breakfast.

After breakfast and feeling a lot better, we were able to find out where the nearest shop was in order to buy some deodorant and other essential supplies.

We were due to be collected and taken back to the airport at 10am that morning, but almost 2 hours later we were still waiting.

At midday a driver finally arrived and back to the airport we went. On arrival at the airport, we were all seated in a specially designated area, and once again made to wait not knowing what was happening, or when we would actually leave.

This time we didn't have long to wait, before we were told our flight would be departing at 2pm that afternoon.

Once we were all seated on the replacement A380 aircraft, the pilot apologised for the delay, blaming it on a faulty door.

I don't know how true this was, as he blamed the

"technical fault" on Airbus, the manufacturer.

Airlines often blame the manufacturer in attempt to absolve themselves of any compensation claims.

Under EU law, EU based airlines are liable if certain factors lead to a delay of more than 4 hours.

In an attempt to avoid having to pay compensation to passengers, airlines often hide behind the manufacturer.

The flight to O.R. Tambo was uneventful, and we landed in Johannesburg at the deserted airport at 2am the next morning.

With a weary sigh of relief we had finally made it to the land of the thinnest toilet paper and some of the fattest government and municipal officials in the world.

I decided there was a common denominator linking the toilet paper and these politicians.

While toilet paper is used mostly for one function, the same item regularly came out of the mouths of these ANC officials.

Day 2

Naturally at that ungodly hour, all shops, banks and cell phone kiosks were closed.

The only advantage arriving at that hour; we did not have to wait long for our baggage, and after collecting our suitcases, went to pick up our rental car.

Having hardly slept on the plane Helen had decided she would be too tired to take part in the Midmar mile as she would still have to drive almost 400 kilometres even if she made it in time to the dam.

I felt sorry for Helen especially as she had spent the previous 5 months each day in the pool making sure she was able to complete the distance within the required time.

It also meant our friends in Durban who were part of the swimming team would be let down. She had sent them an email from the airport in Paris, but with all shops being closed at O.R. Tambo in Johannesburg we were unable to buy a sim card and contact them.

The 550km drive down past the dam and on to Himeville in the Drakensburg was to say the least slow going and mind-numbing for Helen, not to mention to be constantly on the look out for the numerous reckless drivers on the highway.

The first 3 hours on the N3 and in the dark were

particularly stressful, but at least at day break, Helen was able to enjoy the sunrise as the sky turned from black to pink, then orange then a ball of yellow. This made the laborious journey more bearable.

Shortly after 7am, we stopped to have breakfast at a Steers. This was also on our (food places to visit) list.

This burger chain opened for the first time in 1970 in Jeppe Johannesburg.

At present there are over 500 Steers franchises in South Africa and across Africa. There is also a Steers now in London.

As we sat down I said to Helen, "wel Penguin, at least we are more than half way. Hopefully after breakfast and a large strong coffee you will feel slightly better."

"I hope so. I am really tired, and my eyes feel tired, but at least the sun is out."

Helen read out the breakfast menu. It included such titles as; flame-griller breakfast, day braker deluxe, proudly boerie, rise and dine breakfast, flapjack stack, and feel good breakfast.

Helen chose the flame-griller breakfast, which included2 fried eggs, 1 pork banger, and 1 cheese griller, bacon, hand made chips, grilled tomatoe and a slice of toast.

Naturally I went for the proudly boerie breakfast. This included 2 fried eggs, bacon, beef boerewors, Hand made chips, grilled tomatoe and a slice of toast.

While Helen was busy with her second cup of coffee

I asked "Do you want to carry on, or would you rather have a quick nap? Remember there is no hurry to get to Himeville."

"No I feel not too bad. Yes I am quite tired, but would rather get there, and then rest."

"Well when you are ready to leave, let's go."

We paid the bill, and were back on the N3heading for Himeville.

In 1902 Himeville was named after a former road engineer and Prime Minister of Natal, Sir Albert Henry Hime. The town was well-known as a police outpost and a branch of the Border Mounted Rifles in 1890 following a wave of gun-running and cattle rustling in the area.

At the beginning of the last century, the present Museum was once a fort, and later a prison until 1972. Six years later it was declared a national monument.

Since our last visit Helen had decided to invest in a brood of chickens and one rooster.

Her collection started with 5 chickens, which by the time we left had increased to 7 chickens thanks to a neighbour donating 2 hens to add to the brood.

The rooster even though friendly soon became the Bane of my life. It would begin crowing between 3 and 4am each morning even though it was still pitch dark.

I don't know if it was sheer coincidence, but on each previous trip we had never heard a single rooster, but this time no matter where we spent the night, a crowing cockerel could be heard each morning.

I thought to myself at least South African cockerels had the sense to wait until sunrise before they started their crowing.

While the views of the Drakensberg Mountains between Howick and Himeville were at times spectacular, it was also clear to see that the region lacked much investment.

There were many properties for sale, not a good sign for any tourist area.

Those looking for gourmet cuisine in the area will also be disappointed. Most of the restaurants and eateries in the area served what can only be described as basic dishes.

After booking into our hotel, we then had to drive 5 kilometres to Underberg to find a shop selling sim cards.

Once this was done, we returned to Himeville for a quick swim before Helen went for an afternoon nap, while I sat outside enjoying the sound of birds, the fresh air and before long the sound of the Hadeda.

While Helen slept, I thought about a conversation I had overheard at the pool.

Two men from the area were talking about the amount of illegal logging taking place in the area. One of the men said "it's becoming a free for all. The people in charge don't care about the trees; they don't care about all the little hotels which have been forced to close thanks to the state of the roads, these bloody people just don't care, as long as they can screw the country they'll just take ane take until there is nothing left. It's not just the locals, but it won't be long before the Chinese working in Lesotho, who will be doing the same."

It had been over 30 years since I had lived in the area and my band had played at virtually every town in the Drakensburg. It was thriving then, and look what it was like now?

People in Africa blame the British, the French, the Portuguese and the Germans for plundering the continent, but they haven't seen anything yet.

The Chinese will really show them what plunder is all about. Unlike the west today, the Chinese don't care about human rights, corruption and tyranny; they are only too happy to build palaces for the many corrupt leaders while they strip the country of any natural resources. They also tend to employ their own, excluding the locals from any job opportunities.

These environmental rapists will kill any living animal from the biggest to the smallest. From rhinos to the latest reported pilfering; the seahorse.

This has been taking place in Mozambique where they target the local impoverished communities. The Chinese give them a few cents, and get them to catch the seahorse, and once they are dried on a near by beach, the Chinese collect the animals and send them back to China.

Africa let these marauders in at your peril, and by the time you wake up to what is happening, it will be too late; the wildlife and fish stocks will no longer be there.

Another thought occurred to me. Why was it that the

Cape got things right, when it came to tourism, yet here in the Drakensberg, they had failed.

When looking for somewhere to stay, I could not believe how many resorts did not take credit card payments.

My thoughts were interrupted when Helen woke up, and we decided to visit one of the well known farm stalls in the area, but once again, just like the food on offer, we were disappointed. The building was run down, and the goods on offer were not that original.

One thing which did impress me was the honesty box. There was no one serving in the shop, and the owners relied on customer honesty to leave the right amount in the tin after purchasing any items.

I wondered how long this old tradition would last, especially in the "new" South Africa.

After a very ordinary but sufficient meal at the hotel, we were both fast asleep by 7pm. This must have been the earliest I have ever been to bed in the last 30 years.

Day 3

We awoke to the sound of the Hadeda and much to my astonishment the crowing of a rooster in the distance.

Had Helen secretly brought her rooster along with her?

When Helen woke up I interrogated her about this rooster. Did she secretly put that damn rooster in her luggage, or did she organise with the hotel to have a rooster on call just in case I felt home sick?

Helen found the entire rooster episode extremely amusing.

After breakfast we began the 214km journey to Durban. Helen had yet to drive through any township, and I decided instead of taking the N3 highway, we would drive through Edendale, a township on the outskirts of Pietermaritzburg.

During the apartheid years, most of the Zulu families living in the city were moved to Edendale, while the Indian population were moved to Northdale.

It was Sunday morning, and the road to Durban was reasonably quiet. We said goodbye to Himeville and made our way slowly down towards Durban. Helen stopped every now and again to take pictures of the lush green valleys and surrounding mountains and rivers, which she had been too tired to appreciate on our drive up to Himeville.

Edendale much like Africa was a place of contrasts. There were people dressed in their finest on their way to church, and a few yards further on, little boys in rags, while every now and again one could hear the sound of pop music blearing out from a tavern.

Then there were some top of the range cars parked next to jalopies which judging by the looks of them certainly were not road worthy, and of course mini busses. Mini bus taxies in differing states of road worthiness are a feature of the country, especially in all major cities.

The contrast continued with views of some lovely houses and next door to them some shacks.

As we drove through the township we came across cows and goats grazing on the central reservation, seemingly oblivious of the traffic and their human neighbours. Mind you their human neighbours seemed to be oblivious of the cows and goats as well.

We often had to stop while little boys kicked a soccer ball in the main street, also seemingly oblivious or was it more couldn't care less about the traffic passing through their area.

One of the townships most famous residents was Chief Albert Luthuli, Africa's first Nobel Prize winner for peace and former president of the ANC.

Helen found the experience interesting and couldn't get over the contrasts in lifestyles.

With the township behind us, we made our way to Durban and back to my brother's house for a short visit and to say hello to our favourite South African dog gizzy, before visiting the Stables market again, and then on to the Golden Hour market.

Before returning to the digs, we decided to pop in to Chicken licken, the second biggest fast food brand after KFC.

Chicken Licken first opened its doors in 1981 and to date there are over 200 stores.

I had heard about their hot wings, and according to many Talk Radio 702 listeners, these were the best.

Even though Kit was apparently going to hold one of his (braais) barbecue, in the evening, no one knew exactly what time this braai would take place.

The fast food chicken outlet was only 2 blocks away from his house.

Later that evening we caught up on all the news from Kit, his girlfriend Nina, Kim, and the newest resident at the "digs" Rod.

Since our last visit the year before, my brother Kit and Nina had opened a second Thai restaurant.

We couldn't stay up too late as we had to be up and out of the house by 5.45am the next morning to board the Sharks Board boat at 6.30am.

With Gizzie following us, we went to bed.

Day 4

On the previous 2 visits to Durban we had booked to go out on the Sharks Board boat, but due to the weather and lack of other passengers the trip had each time been cancelled.

This time, luck was on our side!! The weather was fine, and there were 7 other passengers ready to visit the shark nets.

We didn't need an alarm clock to wake us up, the Hadeda made sure we were awake, and once again, there was the crow of a rooster in the distance.

Arriving at the launch site with time to spare, and after the skipper signed us in, we were all ready to set sail.

The shark nets are positioned about 400 metres off Shaw, and during our 2 hour trip, the skipper gave a brief talk about the different sharks found in the area, the history of the nets, how the Board tried to save any sharks caught up in the nets and future trends in protecting swimmers.

While out at sea, we saw the crews manning the smaller boats and inspecting the nets for trapped animals and checking the condition of the nets.

Unfortunately over the weekend, a big shark had been trapped in the nets and died. The men from the Sharks board took the body of the 100kg shark further out to sea before dumping it.

The nets are checked each morning during the week, but the boats are not launched over weekends, and this is when most entangled sharks die.

Once back on dry land, we made our way back to the house for breakfast, before deciding how to spend the rest of the day.

We had some shopping to do so decided to get started with the retail therapy later that morning before returning to relax next to the pool.

In the evening we made our annual pilgrimage to Joops restaurant in Durban. This restaurant offers the best steaks on the African continent, and if we never go any where else in Durban, Joops is always a must.

That night at the restaurant we had dinner with one of the former residents at the digs.

Since our last visit, T had got married, and she wanted us to meet her husband.

We all had a wonderful time at Joops, and before we all turned in to pumpkins as the clock rapidly made its way towards midnight, we said our goodbyes and made our way home.

On our way home, we noticed for the second time what can only be described as a new form of begging. The aspiring beggar would kneel in the middle of the road.

"I don't believe it" Helen said as she stopped at a traffic light.

"What don't you believe Penguin?"

"There's a beggar kneeling in the middle of the road!!"

Helen described these beggars as suicide beggars. Were they hoping motorists would stop and give them money, or did they hope a motorist would run over them?

Well, we did neither. There was always the possibility in South Africa, that this was a hoax or ploy by the beggar to rob or highjack the charitable motorist when they stopped to give him some money.

This form of begging was not confined to Durban. We later found these so-called suicide beggars in Johannesburg.

Day 5

Since arriving in KwaZulu-Natal, the temperature had not dropped below 30c, and today was no different.

In the morning we visited the Muthi Market known in Zulu as "Ezinyangeni" or "place of healers". This market next to the well known Victoria street market is the centre in the region for traditional medicine.

The Sangomas (or traditional healers) use many plants, dried skins, and other animal products including Snake skins, baboon parts, vultures, porcupines, crocodile teeth, bird claws, bark and a selection of mysterious powders. The Sangomas believe they have the power to heal, bless or even curse people.

Helen, Kim my photographer and I made our way through the Victoria Street market until we reached the Muthi market.

We were the odd ones out. We were the only white people that morning. As we walked further and deeper into the market, the smell of urine, sweat and herbs was overpowering and as we got closer, the noise from music from giant speakers either side of us reached a Crescendo; the cacophony of sound was deafening.

Within a distance of 20 metres, there must have been at least 50 stands with music bellowing out from them.

The distorted music included traditional, electro pop, and even Christmas carols.

I certainly did not expect to hear carols in the middle of February, but nothing should surprise one in Africa.

Old TVs both black and white and coloured were on sale, along with. Impepho or wild sage, walking sticks, car tyre sandals, plastic wear, many beaded charms and mascots, horse tails, fruit and vegetables, leather belts and sandals, and of course the most popular item in African markets these days air time for cell phones.

On entering the Muthi section of the market, unfortunately none of the stall holders spoke English, however, we did meet a man, who tried to explain to us what each of the pots of different powder were used for. These included healing various ailments, love potions, cures for headaches and any other affliction you might have or might get in the future.

Once out of the general noise and chaos and confusion, we made our way to the more sedate Japanese Gardens, but were disappointed at the state of the park.

It was obvious that municipal officials had decided the Gardens were not a priority even though the gardens urgently needed someTLC.

Helen and I both felt it wouldn't be long before one or other crooked property developer with political connections bought the land and turned it into a housing complex.

At lunch time we went to Kung Thai restaurant in

Umhlanga to meet up with Kit and to sample his food at his second and newest restaurant.

The food was great and we settled for our favourites, the duck pancakes with Thai chilli sauce, and the warm spinach salad.

Standing outside and looking and listening to the dynamic street life, it was hard to believe that not too long ago, this entire area was covered in sugarcane.

Now it is teaming with restaurants, offices and a major shopping mall.

After lunch, it was back to the house for a swim before we had to meet our Midmarfriends, Stuart and Rieva, who we first met 3 years before, and who introduced us to Joops.

Stuart and Rieva had invited us to dinner, and were wonderful hosts. It was great to enjoy a home cooked meal.

Once again, we had to be careful not to turn into pumpkins and before midnight left for home.

Stuart had completed the Midmar mile. We felt terrible. The couple had prepared a picnic for the day, and before the race frantically searched all over for us.

Helen decided she would try for the Midmar mile the following year. However, the next time, we would not fly out with only one day to spare, but rather arrive a week before the race. As they say, and thanks to Air France, once bitten twice shy.

Day 6

The trip to Durban was over, and without fail with each visit we met and made new friends, who insisted we spend time with them on our next trip.

On our way to the northern Drakensburg today about 260 kilometres away, we wanted to stop at Howick to visit the Mandela Monument or as it is known the Mandela Capture Site, which is also the only known monument to a criminal arrest.

It was not easy to find, as the uMngeni municipal authorities have not bothered to clearly sign post the directions.

On August 5, 1962, Nelson Mandela was arrested. He would later be jailed on Robben Island. Mandela was driving past Tweedie with MK member Cecil Williams when he was arrested by the police.

We drove along the R103 and turned down a side road where we eventually found the monument.

It consists of 50 steel columns each between 6.5 and 9.5 metres tall forming a portrait of Nelson Mandela against the backdrop of rolling hills and valleys.

An additional five smaller columns create an axis from the main sculpture to the monument site across the road.

Locals also believe the near by bench played its

part that day. They believe Mandela sat on the bench, before he was taken to prison.

Many people don't know that Howick was also the site of one of the many concentration camps set up by the British during the Anglo-Boer War from 1899 to 1902.

After Helen took some pictures of the monument, we continued our journey along the more scenic route instead of going back to the N3 highway.

That afternoon we reached the guest house at Geluksburg near Bergville. The village is close to the famous ""Lost Valley "" in the Drakensberg which has its own place in the folklore of the Drakensberg. It is the site of a "white tribe", which lived isolated from the rest of civilisation until just after the turn of the century. It is a unique geographical area, repeated only at Die Hell near Outshoorn.

Another feature of the area is a man-made suspension bridge, still in working order at the bottom of the 4x4 Trail into Lost Valley. A statue, the 'Kaalvoet Vrou", stands close to Retief's Pass and Voortrekker Pass, commemorating the 1837 entry into Natal by Retief, one of its voortrekker leaders.

Before the Europeans arrived, the San or Bushmen first populated this area of the Drakensberg. Over 4000 Bushman paintings can still be found in caves and cliff overhangs.

The Bushmen are believed to have been exterminated in the 1800's by farmers and bounty hunters.

I had found the guest house on the internet before we left, and the owner Penny had kindly offered to cook us dinner when we got there, and she said it wouldn't cost a lot more.

Just as well we took up her offer. The nearest restaurant was about 30 kilometres away down a gravel road.

We met Penny's mother, who with her husband had moved out from Newcastle in the UK in the 80s, and after buying the land, her husband began building.

The grandmother told us her husband had a passion for building, and since 1987, he had built not only the main house, but another 24 guest units.

We also got to meet the family dog, Peanut a friendly Labrador.

Dinner that evening was very good, and so was breakfast the next morning.

I wondered if I would get to hear the Hadeda, and more so a rooster.

Sure enough, I heard both before breakfast.

Day 7

After a leisurely breakfast, we packed our suitcases in the car and made our way towards Johannesburg some 380 kilometres away via Van reenen's Pass, which is half way between Durban and the city of gold.

This had become a favourite tea room for Helen, and each time we found ourselves on the N3, we would stop off and have a cup of tea and one of their delicious cakes.

We had also got to know the owner's dog, and this time, she had fostered another 4-legged friend.

Not only are the cakes a treat, but the tearoom also includes a well stocked shop with many home-made products.

Having paid our respects to the tea room, we continued our journey to the city of gold.

Arriving in Johannesburg late that afternoon, and after checking in to the guest house in Northcliff were soon greeted by a typical Johannesburg thunder storm.

There was thunder and lightning and a torrential downpour with hale for all of about 20 minutes; before it suddenly stopped, and apart from the standing water, you would never have guessed it had rained.

Northcliff manor was one of the earliest homes built in the area, and was also a wedding gift to Ms Helen Suzmann, the well known anti-apartheid politician. She was the Progressive Party's only representative for 13 years in an intimidating Afrikaans and male dominated apartheid parliament.

During her lifetime she was awarded 27 honorary doctorates and made an honorary Dame Commander of the Order of The British Empire.

She was also nominated twice for the Nobel peace Prize. Sadly, at the age of 91 years old, she died on New Years Day 2009, but her fight against apartheid lives on.

The owners Johnny and Ilse van der Merwe are award winning designers and manufacturers of stage, film and TV décor sets since the beginning of the South African television industry. Ilse is also a well known artist, and some of her pieces can be seen at the guesthouse.

Thanks to Johnny, the manor also boasts many European Antiques and Yellow- and Stinkwood Africana Furniture as well as a collection of Victorian glass and Italian furniture.

We were assigned the Gold Room described as Sunny, a gold and black antique French themed room with balcony and beautiful views.

While the views of the landscaped gardens did not benefit me, I did enjoy sitting each morning on the balcony and listening to the birds.

Before we went out for a meal that night, we met with one of the local designers. Helen had ordered some cushion covers, bags and material. Frances Helen and I sat and chatted outside on the veranda for about one hour. We were joined outside by a German tourist, who had also arrived that afternoon.

He was spending a couple of days at the guest house before setting out on a safari.

We asked him if he wanted to join us at the restaurant, and shortly after Frances left, the 3 of us set off to the restaurant.

The meal at the Thunder Gun, a well known family restaurant reporting to offer the best hamburgers in the city was great.

Helen and I each had a hamburger, and our German friend a 500g t-bone steak.

After returning to the guesthouse we made our way to our rooms for the night.

Day 8

The next morning, I woke up to the call of the Hadeda, the cool refreshing air of Johannesburg, and Believe it or not, someone in the area had a rooster.

During what was a lovely breakfast we met the owners Johnny and Ilse.

Nearing the end of our breakfast Ilse walked in and asked me "How do you know where your mouth is?"

It is not often I am left speechless and flabbergasted.

With thoughts rushing through my head I thought what an incredibly stupid and pathetic question.

A moment of silence followed, before I replied "Do you look at where your mouth is when eating?"

Another moment of silence followed, before she said "No, I guess not."

Later that morning, we set off for the Peace shop in The Firs in Rosebank. We had ordered several hand made items, and the owner Eugenie had kept them for us.

After spending about one hour at the shop and looking at the display of wooden and felt animals it was time to leave, and make our way to a couple of supermarkets and chain stores.

In the afternoon, we returned to the guest house and Helen went to sleep for a couple of hours, while I sat outside and enjoyed the serenity. It was hard to believe we were in this aggressive and fast paced city.

Since our first trip, I had noticed how many things had changed. There were many more black people eating in restaurants and spending their money in shops.

Many of the jobs previously held by whites were now the domain of black people.

The listenership on radio had also changed. This was most noticeable on Talk Radio 702. I would guess that over a 24 hour period 75% of the callers were black listeners. There were also more black presenters on air. I wondered how long some of the white presenters would last, especially those who could not speak one of the black languages.

Another radio station which had dramatically changed was SAFM. This station was previously the realm of whites. Now it was almost exclusively black listeners and black presenters.

One station that had not changed much was Cape Talk 567, the sister station of 702. It seemed to still attract primarily white listeners.

In the evening we went to the Barnyard theatre to see a tribute show performed by several local musicians.

Day 9

After a coffee, and the call of a Hadeda and a rooster, it was time for breakfast, and to pack our bags ready for the 410 kilometre trip to Hazyview.

We decided instead of taking the monotonous highway, we would drive through Belfast, Dullstroom, and on to Hazyview.

Stopping at Dullstroom we browsed through some of the specialty shops and a farm stall.

These shops were certainly better than anything we had previously found in the Drakensberg, and one quickly noticed how the town was geared towards tourists especially those who enjoyed trout fishing, judging on the amount of fishing shops.

Our chosen route took us past lydenburg and on to and over the long tom pass where we stopped a couple of times so Helen could take some pictures.

Reaching the top, a large silver cannon called The Long Tom can still be found. This was the British name for the Boer-operated field gun that fired a 38kg shell for 10km and was the curse of British generals and their brigades.

Once over and down the pass, it was on to our guest house on the outskirts of Hazyview.

The rooms at the resort were fine, and the views from them spectacular, but we felt the German owners were more interested in fleecing tourists than genuine hospitality.

Unlike most other guest houses, instead of a welcoming cup of coffee and fruit juice, we had to pay for a cold drink and a bottle of water.

At dinner that night, the owners told us the municipal water was unsafe to drink, and we would have to pay for bottled water, but later we questioned several residents in the area, who told us there was nothing wrong with the water. So who do you believe?

While the buffet breakfast at the resort was great, the 3 course meal that evening was second-rate. The cheapest cuts of meat and the cheapest ingredients were used.

I sent my main meal back pointing out I would need a chainsaw to cut the meat.

Admittedly the owners offered a refund or an invitation to join them the following evening for free, but as they say, once bitten twice shy.

We also discovered that for the same price, we could get a really good meal at one of the many top quality restaurants in the area.

Before we went to bed that first night, we collected our packed breakfast from the guest house to take with us on our day long game drive the next morning.

Day 10

oday we would be going on a guided game drive to the world renowned Kruger National park, and it would be Helen's last chance to see a leopard in the wild.

As we were about to leave the resort at 4.45, we were greeted by the call of the Hadeda and you guessed it, a rooster crowing, and a couple of minutes later by our guide, Frances.

We had to be at the gate to the Park when it opened at 5.30am. When we got there in our open 4x4 vehicle, Frances first had to fill in the various permits, before we were allowed to enter.

Documentation completed and off we went in search of the elusive and nocturnal leopard, and in fact to find any animals.

One of the advantages we soon discovered about going on an organized game drive with a major company; each vehicle was fitted with a 2-way radio.

This allowed the guide to keep in touch with other vehicles in the fleet, which alerted them to various sightings.

While a self-drive is optional, I doubt if you would see as many animals. You wouldn't have the benefit of knowing where some of the animals had been spotted.

The advantage of a guide soon became apparent, when

the silence was broken and the radio came to life, with guides across the Park letting their colleagues know what they had found.

A voice on the radio told Frances that he had spotted 3 lion cubs on a rock some distance from one of the roads.

We immediately made our way to the site, and true enough, there were the lion cubs.

It didn't take us long to spot the ever present impala, a couple of kudu, some giraffe, zebra, and some solitary elephants. We also saw some vultures perched in a tree.

Of more interest to me were the new and different bird calls, which I had not heard before and in particular the woodland kingfisher, with its bright blue feathers on its back, wings and tail, and black shoulders and a white belly. It has a red and black beak, and seemed to be everywhere.

Frances told me that this bird from North Africa is found in this part of the Kruger during the summer months. She said it does not catch and eat fish, but loves to hunt insects on the ground.

Before we knew it, it was 9.30am, and breakfast called. We made our way to Skukuza one of the camps inside the Park.

The camp is very commercial, with a bank, post office, petrol station, restaurant, and curio shops.

While Helen grabbed a cup of coffee from the restaurant, one of the visitors claimed he came across a leopard kill. Our only sighting of a kill at that stage was a grasshopper been eaten by a bird.

We went outside, unpacked and ate our breakfast, while waiting for Frances to call us to continue our game viewing.

As soon as we drove out of the camp, the radio came to life and one of the guides said he had spotted a leopard on one of the rocks about 3 kilometres away.

Helen's heart leapt for joy. May be she would get lucky and finally see the animal, one of the last of the big 5 which had until now evaded her.

We made our way to the rock formation, and as we took our position between 6 other vehicles we stopped and switched off the engine to wait and watch.

The leopard was about 200 metres away lying on a rock.

Waiting, no one daring to speak, it sat up, stretched, and slowly made its way down the rock.

The three of us sat silently as it made its way towards the parked vehicles, and suddenly turned and walked right in front of our vehicle.

Helen and frances could hardly believe what they had witnessed.

"I can't believe it!!! Did you see it walked straight in front of our vehicle? How lucky I am!!I could see it on the rocks, but never thought it would get that close, and even better, walk in front of us." Helen said excitedly.

After the leopard disappeared into the bush, we set off again, and about 15 minutes later turning a corner, we found 3 cheetahs making their way across the road. This was also a rare sighting.

A leopard and 3 cheetahs in one day, could things get any better?

The next sighting was a dwarf mongoose followed by a tortoise, and then an Elephant which couldn't have been more than a metre away from us, while it gracefully munched its way through Marulas.

Once again, we stopped and we all remained silent, not wishing to disturb the animal.

I could actually hear it eating, it was that close.

There was yet another first for Helen as we continued our safari. It was a termite mound, or as we called them ant hills.

This ant hill was at least 7 metres high, and had probably taken scores of years to reach that height.

The termites or ants inhabiting such a structure are divided into different categories. There are the workers, who are blind, then the soldiers, who protect and fight, and then there is the queen and king ant.

After that we went on to Khandzalive hill, the highest point in the Park where we got out to stretch our legs. Frances showed Helen Gods Window in the distance. While we stood outside, I could feel and sense the vastness of the Park.

As Helen admired the 360 degrees view, a bateleur eagle circled overhead.

By the time we returned to Skukuza at about 1pm for

lunch, Helen and Frances were still talking about the Leopard and the Cheetahs they saw.

One hour later we were back on the road, and on our final leg of the Kruger.

Frances drove down to a near by dam, where Helen saw Buffalo, Hippo, Impala, and a single Rhino.

On our way out we came across another Giraffe, and a female Elephant and her calf, as well as a loan Steenbok.

The Steenbok is one of the smallest buck weighing about 10kg. And the only buck which digs a hole before doing its business, before covering it up with sand.

Back at the guest house, we went for a swim, before returning to Hazyview to find somewhere to eat that night.

The restaurant we chose allowed us to sit outside under the shade of a Marula tree. This might have looked like a lovely setting, but we soon found out why no other patrons had chosen the table.

Every now and again a rock hard Marula fruit would suddenly drop from the tree on to the floor narrowly missing us.

After the meal we made our way back to the guest house trying to avoid the numerous potholes in the road.

While locals didn't seem to mind the potholes, and probably knew where they were, it was more difficult for Helen, a stranger in the area, and not only that, but it was dark when we drove back.

She would have to suddenly swerve in an attempt to avoid each pothole.

Day 11

Today would be a relaxing day with nothing on our to do list.

After breakfast we made our way back to hazyview to first find a laundry mat, then on to visit some of the shops.

We had decided to do a boat trip the next day, but when we got to the booking agency, were told the boat did not leave on Tuesdays. We would have to find something else to do the next day.

Driving back towards the guest house that afternoon we passed fields of bananas and mangos before reaching a coffee shop.

This was a coffee shop with a difference. Not only could you have a cup of coffee, but you could also watch as they roasted the coffee beans from a near by plantation.

After the roasting demonstration and a cup of coffee and a cake, we made our way back to the guest house to relax next to the pool.

Before we knew it, the sun was setting, and the time had come to drive back to Hazyview to find and try out another restaurant.

The restaurant we chose once again allowed us to sit outside, but this time it was next to a water feature and stream.

Unfortunately, perched on a rock in the stream sat a spider, which according to Helen only had eyes for her.

Helen as you already know has a fear of spiders, no matter the size.

I suggested she change seats, and have her back to the gawking spider, but this she said would be even worse.

"At least where I am sitting, I can keep an eye on that spider."

For the second night running we both chose to have a steak, while Helen had a crème brulee and I had a dom pedro.

The meal was excellent, but Helen said after we left, she was unable to relax, even though she too enjoyed the food.

Back again along the dangerous road to the guest house, and fortunately, no accident.

Day 12

Our final full day in the area, and we were going to visit Moholoholo WildLife Rehabilitation Centre.

It would take us about 3 hours to get there, so after breakfast we set off for the centre.

Moholoholo WildLife Centre is home to various animals and birds which have been abandoned injured or poisoned. If at all possible rehabilitated birds and animals are returned to the wild, but those less fortunate are kept at the centre and help in educating the public.

The centre was established in 1992 by Johan Strijdom, owner and wildlife enthusiast, along with Brian Jones, a pioneer in wildlife conservation throughout South Africa.

To quote The aims of Moholoholo are "To create homes for orphaned, poisoned or injured wildlife that will never be able to return to their natural environment as a result of their circumstances or injuries. If possible To reintroduce rehabilitated wildlife to their natural environment. To establish breeding facilities for our wildlife and to reintroduce their offspring back into the wild.

By means of our educational programme, emphasise how sensitive and fragile our ecosystem is and how fast we are losing it. To join hands with any other conservation group that shares our objective of conserving our natural heritage."

The centre also has a volunteer student programme. Apart from the daily activities, volunteers will be taken after hours on bush walks, night drives, sleep outs and big five picnics. The luckly volunteer might even get to sleep under the stars on a "big five" game farm.

Breakfast lunch and dinner are all provided and staff and volunteers sit together at these meals.

I would say another aim of the centre is to create a happy family between staff, volunteers and the animals.

When we got to the gate and signed in, the first animal we saw in the grounds was a young giraffe. According to the staff, the Giraffe thought he was a human, and we were told not to approach him.

After parking the car, we went inside and were all told about the history of Moholoholo, before we began the tour.

Our African guide told us about each of the animals, as well as also about the various African myths and the parts of animals used in these beliefs.

We saw several birds of pray, and I got to stroke a bateleur eagle. Other residents included lions, 2 leopards, hyenas, a Honey Badger, a Serval cat, a cheetah, which we were able to touch and stroke, and several different vultures.

Towards the end of the tour we all made our way to the vulture restaurant. Those who wanted and were brave enough could feed the patrons.

A special full length glove was put over your arm, and

then a piece of meat placed on top of your hand. Before you knew it, one of the vultures would fly down, land on your arm, and take the meat.

At this invitation, I immediately volunteered. After putting on the glove, and the meat resting on my hand, one of the Cape Vultures flew down, and all 14kgs of the bird sat on my arm until I lowered it, and it flew on to the ground.

What a privilege, and yet, people willingly and deliberately kill this beautiful bird.

I don't know who is worse, the Vietnamese and Chinese wanting the Rhino horn or people in Africa killing birds and other animals for their archaic and utterly meaningless beliefs. The so-called properties attributed to these animals are laughable and without any basis.

The government should start by educating its own people, before worrying about foreigners and their unfounded myths. Instead they stand by and do nothing to protect many of these animals and use culture and tradition as a feeble excuse.

Brian Jones believed "Africa is finished. Animals, birds, trees, bushes and herbs are all under threat.

If anyone tells you anything else, bring them to me, and I will call them stupid."

These predictions by Brian had some truth about them. Much of southern Angola was already completely devoid of wild life, along with many trees and birds. The same could be said about parts of Zimbabwe, no doubt Mozambique to follow along with numerous other African countries.

How long would it be before much that Africa had to offer would be lost for ever thanks to lack of people education, its leaders benefiting from illegal trade in animal parts and the latest threat to any and all natural resources and the environment; the Chinese.

On our way back to Hazyview, we noticed a sign saying "Wales", but there was no clue about the destination or what it was supposed to indicate.

Arriving back in the town, we decided to have dinner at one of the town's best steak houses.

Once again, we found ourselves next to a water feature and a stream.

Fortunately for Helen, there was no spider to keep its watchful eyes over her. This time we were joined by several frogs, who kept up their steady calling.

After the meal it was back to the guest house, and once again luckily we did not hit any potholes.

Our stay in the area had come to an end, and the next morning it would be back to Johannesburg.

Day 13

We were keen to be on the road and after an early breakfast left via the Long tom pass stopping at Dullstroom to do some last minute shopping.

Before we went back to Northcliff manor, we popped in to The thunder gun again for a late lunch.

Back at Northcliff manor, we spent the remainder of the afternoon relaxing next to the pool, before it was time to drive to the theatre at Montecasino.

Helen had booked tickets to see the Rocky Horror show that evening.

The show was world class, and we thoroughly enjoyed the performance by the cast.

Day 14

It was our last day, and the last time to hear the Hadeda and not forgetting the rooster in the distance.

After breakfast we packed and weighed our suitcases, before leaving to do some final shopping.

Later that morning we went to Liliesleaf Farm. This is where many of the ANC leadership were arrested in the early 60s, which in turn lead to the Rivonia trial.

It had been a safe house for many of the leaders, and where Mandela had previously lived under the assumed name of David Motsamayi as a farm worker.

On 11 July 1963, during the final meeting at this venue, security police raided the farm and arrested 19 members of the movement, charging them with sabotage.

Mandela who was already in prison was charged along with the Rivonia 19 suspects, when the police found numerous documents incriminating him.

We both found it extremely interesting to listen and in Helen's case to watch various interviews carried out by the researchers of the farm.

There were two stories which I found hard to believe. The first was a young child, who allegedly took down various number plate registrations of cars visiting the farm, and handed them to the police. The other hard to believe story was that of a neighbor, who finding a "black man" in the lounge speaking to a "white man" reported the sighting to the police.

This is definitely one of the places to visit if you are in Johannesburg.

After the trip to Liliesleaf Farm we went back to the guesthouse to collect our suitcases, and head out to the Lion Park.

Apart from viewing lions and cheetahs, and various buck, two of the other highlights included a brief interaction with some lion cubs, and a chance to feed a giraffe while standing on a platform.

I sat and had a cup of coffee, while Helen went to do both. She came back about 15 minutes later overjoyed at the experience.

As she said, many people might have seen a giraffe, but how many had actually hand-fed a giraffe?

Our final stop before returning to the airport was Carnivores restaurant, which we had visited at the end of our very first trip to the country.

What a better way to complete my big five adventure as I tucked into some impala, hartebeest, crocodile, kudu and wildebeest cuts of meat.

As we drove to the airport, I thought to my self sadly my big five adventure was over, but at least, Helen had got to see at close hand the big five.

During our 5 trips, she visited and saw many of the popular shops which most South Africans from all walks of life spent their money in.

These included Woolworths, Pick n Pay, Checkers, Spar, Foschini, Truworths, Edgars, Donna Claire, Milady's, Jet, Ackermans, Pep stores, Cape Union Mart as well as the four Mr Price outlets.

She also visited some of the biggest shopping malls as well as the smallest spaza shops.

Unlike most tourists, who spent their money at the many exclusive restaurants and maybe time at international branded stores, Helen was able at first hand to get to know and feel part of South Africa.

This book is dedicated to Helen or as I called her, Penguin, who became part of me and part of my life for over 10 years.

Even though I love the country, I doubt some how if I would have returned so many times, if it had not been for Helen. Looking back, it was well worth it. There is nothing better and more rewarding than sharing precious moments with that special person in your life, especially if those moments are in a special country.

South African Recipes

Thanks to the kind permission of Peter Thomas, the recipes I have included below can be found along with numerous other past and present South African treats on www.funkymunky.co.za

This site probably has the most comprehensive list of traditional South African recipes.

Traditional Milk Tart

7 ml butter

1 ml salt

25 ml cinnamon

750 ml boiling milk

10 ml custard powder

15 ml cornflour or maizena

15 ml cake flour

25 ml cold milk

125 ml white sugar

4 large eggs, separated

2 ml vanilla extract

Cinnamon sugar (5 ml ground cinnamon for every 65 ml sugar)

500 g puff or flaky pastry, if you don't want to make the pastry from scratch.

Method

Line 2 pie plates with the pastry and make a raised edge for each. For the filling, add butter, salt and cinnamon to boiling milk. Mix the custard powder, cornflour and flour to a paste with the cold milk. Stir in a little of the hot milk mixture. Stir the custard mixture into the hot milk, add 50 ml of the sugar and bring to the boil, stirring continuously. Remove from the stove when it has thickened and discard the cinnamon stick. Beat the egg whites until stiff but not dry. Gradually beat in the remaining sugar. Beat the egg yolks lightly and stir in a little of the custard mixture. Stir the yolks into the custard mixture then add the almond essence. Gradually fold in the egg whites. Pour the mixture into the pastry cases and bake at 200 C for approx 10 minutes. Lower the temperature to 180 C and bake for a further 10 to 15 minutes or until the filling has set. Cool slightly and sprinkle the tart with cinnamon sugar.

Crustless Milk Tart

4 eggs, separated

250 ml sugar

75 ml melted butter melted

250 ml, unsifted cake flour

5ml baking powder

pinch of salt

1litre milk

5ml vanilla essence

50 ml) cinnamon sugar (ground cinnamon mixed with sugar)

Method

Preheat oven to 180°C (350°F).

Grease tart pans with non-stick spray

Beat egg yolks, sugar and butter till creamy. Sift cake flour, baking powder and salt together and beat it into the egg mixture. Add milk and vanilla essence and mix.

Beat egg whites till firm and fold into milk mixture with a metal spoon; the mixture is thin. Pour mixture into tart pans and bake for 40 - 50 minutes on middle oven shelf till done.

Serve hot or cold.

Tipsy tart

Batter:

250 g stoned dates, chopped

5 ml bicarbonate of soda

250 ml boiling water

375 ml cake flour

2 ml baking powder

pinch salt
125 g butter, at room temperature
250 ml white sugar
2 extra-large eggs
100 g walnuts, chopped
100 g glace cherries, halved
Sauce:
15 ml butter
190 ml brown sugar
250 ml water
3 ml vanilla essence
125 ml brandy

Method

Preheat the oven to 180 °C. Butter a 27 cm ovenproof dish with butter or spray with non-stick spray. Place the dates and bicarbonate of soda in a mixing bowl and pour over the boiling water. Set aside to cool. Sift the cake flour, baking powder and salt together. Cream the butter and sugar together until light and creamy and add the eggs one at a time, beating well after each addition. Sift the dry ingredients on top and add the nuts and cherries. Add the dates, stirring until well mixed. Turn the batter into the prepared dish and bake for 45-50 minutes or until a testing skewer comes out clean. Meanwhile heat the butter, sugar and water for the sauce in a saucepan until the sugar has dissolved. Bring to the boil and reduce the sauce until it turns syrupy. Remove from the heat and stir in the vanilla essence and brandy. Pour the sauce over the hot tart as soon as it comes out of the oven. Serve lukewarm or at room temperature with custard or whipped cream. Serves 8-10

Peppermint fridge tart

Other main ingredients for a fridge tart could be coffee, banana, pineapple,

Caramel, Cassata, Chocolate, Coconut,

And Lemon.

1 tin caramel treat or 1 tin condensed milk caramelized tennis biscuits

1 box oley whip

1 slab peppermint chocolate

1 peppermint crisp

Method

Whip oley whip with hand mixture until stiff. Add caramel treat and mix. Then grate peppermint slab and mix. Layer tennis biscuits in fridge tart dish (long in length) and add mixture. Grate peppermint crisp chocolate on top. Refrigerate try and make it the night before.

Wildebeeskastaiings: An old version of koeksisters

Syrup:

200g white sugar

250ml water
5ml lemon juice
25ml golden syrup
Batter:
300g cake flour
12.5ml baking powder
1ml salt
12.5ml butter
2 eggs beaten
100 ml milk
cornflour
extra butter, softened
sunflower oil for deep frying

Method

Syrup: Bring the syrup ingredients to the boil and stir until all the sugar has dissolved. Cook syrup for 8 minutes over moderate heat. Let it cool then put it in the fridge till its ice cold.

Batter: Sift the flour, baking powder and salt together. Rub the 12.5 ml of butter into the mixture. Beat the eggs and milk together and cut this mixture into the flour mixture with a spatula. Add a little extra milk if the dough is too stiff.

Shape the dough into a sausage and divide it into 6 equal lengths. Roll each length into a thin oval shape on a flour strewn surface.. Spread softened butter on the dough ovals and sprinkle them with cornflour. Stack the ovals on top of each other until you have a stack of 6 ovals.

Now roll the stack out into a thin rectangle. Roll up the rectangle tightly lengthwise. Using a sharp knife, cut the roll into 2 cm slices. Moisten the ends of each little roll and press them together to prevent the roll from unraveling when they're fried. Fry a few rolls at a time in moderately hot, deep, sunflower oil till they're golden brown. Remove from oil with a slotted spoon and dip them immediately in the ice-cold syrup. Drain on a wire rack on a tray. Chill before serving, makes about 50.

Koeksisters

The secret of the crisp syrupy outside of koeksisters is that they are taken straight from hot oil and dipped into ice-cold syrup. This seals the syrup outside and leaves the inside dryish in contrast.

375ml water

800g sugar

2ml (1/2t) cream of tartar

2ml (1/2t) ground ginger

3 cinnamon sticks

500g cake flour

30ml (6t) baking powder

2ml (1/2t) salt

50ml (4T0 butter or margarine

2 eggs

250ml milk

oil for deep frying

Method

To make syrup, heat water in a saucepan, add sugar and stir until dissolved. Add cream of tartar, ginger and cinnamon.

Boil, uncovered, for 5 minutes. Do not stir, remove from stove and chill.

While syrup is chilling, make koeksisters. Sift flour, baking powder and salt together.

Add butter and rub in with fingertips until mixture resembles fine crumbs.

Beat eggs and milk together and add to dry ingredients. Mix dough well, then knead lightly for 2 minutes to make it pliable.

Cover basin with wax paper and leave for 1 hour.

Roll dough to a thickness of 7.5 to 10mm. Cut into strips about 8 cm long and 2.5 cm wide. Cut each strip into three lengthwise, leaving one side uncut. Now plait the three pieces and press ends together firmly.

Heat oil to 190°C and deepfry koeksisters for 1 minute. (Do not fry too many at once)

The syrup will warm up about halfway through, so divide the syrup into two bowls.

Remove from oil, drain on brown paper for 1 minute and dip in cold syrup for 30 seconds. Remove from syrup and place on a dish to dry.

Cape Malay Koeksisters with coconut

250 ml (1 cup) cake flour

250 ml (1 cup) self raising flour
5 ml (1 tsp) salt
60g (1/4 cup) butter
5 ml (1tsp) ground ginger
5 ml (1 tsp) ground cinnamon
5 ml (1 tsp) ground mixed spice
2.5 ml (1/2 tsp) ground cardamom
10 ml (2 tsp) soft brown sugar
10 ml (2 tsp) white sugar
7.5 ml (1 1/2 tsp) instant dry yeast
375 ml (1 1/2 cups) warm water
Syrup:
250ml (1 cup) water
125ml (1/2 cup) sugar
15ml (1 tbsp) dessicated coconut
1 piece of naartjie peel

Method

In a mixing bowl combine the flours with salt. Add butter and rub in lightly till it resembles fine breadcrumbs. Add remaining ingredients, using the warm water to form a dough. Do not knead. Cover with plastic and leave in a warm place fo0r about 1/1/2 to 2 hours or until doubled in size then turn out on a lightly floured surface.

Dip fingers and knife into flour and use your hands to stretch the dough. Cut into 4cm X8cm strips and deep fry over medium heat in a deep saucepan. Insert fork to check if done, and remove quickly one by one and drain in colander or on kitchen paper.

To make the syrup bring, water, sugar, coconut and naartjie peel to a slow boil in a large saucepan until syrup starts to bubble.

Prick each koeksister, then lower into syrup . Add as many koeksisters as the pan will hold. Turn and cook for 5 minutes each side or till browned. Remove with slotted spoon place on platter with some extra coconut. Sprinkle coconut over them and serve while hot

Cape brandy pudding

250 g dates, stoned and finely chopped
5 ml bicarbonate of soda
250 ml boiling water
125 g margarine
200 g sugar
2 eggs, beaten
240 g cake flour
5 ml baking powder
2 ml salt
250 ml walnuts or pecan nuts, chopped
Sauce:
300 ml sugar
15 ml butter
200 ml water
5 ml vanilla essence
2 ml salt
25 ml brandy

Method

Preheat oven to 180 °C.

1. Divide chopped dates into 2 portions. Add bicarbonate of soda and boiling water to 1 portion, mix well and leave to cool.

2. Cream margarine and sugar then beat in eggs.

3. Sift flour, baking powder and salt over mixture and fold in. Add dry portions of dates and walnuts, blending well.

4. Stir in bicarbonate of soda mixture, blend thoroughly and turn batter out into a large baking dish. Bake for 40 minutes or until firm.

Sauce:

Heat sugar, butter and water for 5 minutes. Remove from stove and stir in vanilla essence, salt and brandy. Pour sauce over pudding as soon as it comes out of the oven and serve hot or cold with whipped cream.

Malva Pudding

1 cup flour

1 tablespoon bicarbonate of soda

1 cup sugar

1 egg

1 tablespoon apricot jam

1 tablespoon vinegar

1 tablespoon melted butter

1 cup milk.

For the sauce:
½ cup cream
½ cup milk
1 cup sugar
½ cup hot water
½ cup butter

Method

Butter an ovenproof glass or porcelain container. Sift the flour and bicarb into a bowl and stir in the sugar. In another bowl beat the egg very well and add the other ingredients (excluding those for the sauce) one by one, beating well. Using a wooden spoon beat the wet ingredients into the dry.

Pour batter into the baking dish, cover with greased foil, greased side down, and bake in a 180°C preheated oven for 45 minutes until well risen and for another 5 minutes if not browned enough.

If not sufficiently baked the pudding won't absorb the sauce making it stodgy inside.

When almost done, heat the ingredients for the sauce making sure all the sugar and butter are melted. When the pudding is done, remove from the oven, pour over the sauce. Serve hot or at room temperature with a little cream.

Traditional Smoorsnoek

Buy some smoked snoek or any nice white smoked fish

will work as a substitute.

30ml oil

40g butter

2 onions, sliced

3 potatoes, diced

1 400g tin whole chopped tomatoes, use juice as well (this is optional)

15 ml sugar

Garlic and Chilli(optional)

250g smoked snoek, skinned, carefully boned and flaked

freshly cut lemon for squeezing on afterwards

Method

Sauté the sliced onion in the oil and butter mixture. Add the diced potatoes and stir-fry until golden. Add tomatoes, sugar and seasoning. Simmer gently until the potatoes are cooked.

Add snoek and heat through.

Bobotie a meat loaf smothered in a golden savory egg topping.

2 slices stale white bread (remove the crusts)

30ml cooking oil

1 onion, thinly sliced

2,5ml ground cloves

5ml crushed garlic

3ml salt

10 ml curry powder

5 ml turmeric
500g beef or lamb mince
2 eggs
30ml hot water
20ml lemon juice
25ml sugar
Topping:
1 egg (lightly beaten)
150ml milk
bay or lemon leaves for garnishing

Method

Preheat oven to 160°C. Soak bread in water for 10 minutes, squeeze out excess water and crumble. In a large frying pan, heat oil and braise onion until golden (about 7 minutes). Add the ground cloves, garlic, salt, curry powder and turmeric and simmer for 5 minutes. Break the 2 eggs into a large bowl and beat lightly. Mix in the mince. Add the onion mixture from the frying pan to the mince as well as the hot water, lemon juice, crumbled bread and sugar, and mix to combine well. Spoon the mixture into a well greased oven proof dish and bake for 40 minutes or until golden brown. Remove from the oven.

Topping: Combine the egg or for a thicker topping add buttermilk or yogurt, and beat well. Pour over the bobotie. Arrange bay leaves or lemon leaves as garnish. Return to oven and bake at 180°C for 5-10 minutes, or until topping is set.

Sosaties - kebabs with a unique South African flavour!

1kg lamb cut into 1" pieces

500g pork cut into ½" cubes

You can also use beef or chicken.

Other ingredience include 1 garlic clove, peeled

Salt, pepper

4 tbsp oil

1 cup onions, chopped

1 tbsp curry powder

1 clove garlic, minced

2 tbsp sugar

1 tbsp tamarind paste

2 cups white vinegar

2 tbsp apricot jam

2 tbsp cornstarch dissolved in

2 tbsp red wine

½ pound dried apricots

½ cup dry sherry(optional)

Method

1. Place the lamb and pork pieces in a large bowl that has been rubbed with the clove of garlic.

2. Season with salt and pepper, and toss.

3. In a saucepan, heat the oil. Add the onions and sautè for 5-6 minutes, then add the curry powder and garlic.

4. Sautè for another minute. Add the sugar, tamarind paste, vinegar, and jam and stir well.

5. Stir the cornstarch mixture and add it to the onions, and cook, stirring constantly, until it thickens.

6. This should take about 3 minutes. Cool, then add to the meat and toss well. Marinate for 2-3 days.

7. One day before preparing the sosaties, combine the dried apricots and sherry in a small bowl, cover, and let sit overnight in the refrigerator.

8. Drain meat from sauce and reserve. Thread lamb, pork, and apricots on skewers.

9. Grill over charcoal until browned on all sides. Serve with heated marinating sauce.

Curry oxtail stew

1.5 kg oxtail

30 ml curry powder

4 cloves

4 peppercorns

1 bay leaf

250-500 ml meat stock

1 small onion, sliced

1 carrot, chopped

1 turnip, chopped

butter

30 ml cake flour

Method

Cut the oxtail into joints and wash thoroughly.

Place meat in a heavy saucepan and add the spices and

boiling water.

Simmer for three to four hours, adding more stock when necessary.

After two hours add salt, pepper, onion, carrot and turnip.

Remove spices and skim off as much fat as possible.

Melt the butter in a pan, add the cake flour and fry until brown.

Add the flour mixture to the meat and gravy in the saucepan and stir until the gravy thickens.

Simmer for 15 minutes.

Serve with rice or mashed potatoes.

Boerewors

A spicy sausage that no self respecting South african can go without on a barbecue

There are many variants on this traditional sausage, but the basic recipe remains the same.

1.5kg beef

1.5kg pork

500g bacon, diced(optional)

25ml salt

5ml ground pepper

50ml ground coriander

2ml freshly grated nutmeg

1ml ground cloves

2ml ground dried thyme(optional)

2ml ground allspice

125ml vinegar

1 clove garlic, crushed

50ml Worcestershire sauce

85g sausage casings

Method

1. Cut the beef and pork meat into 1.5 " cubes and mix it with all the other ingredients except the sausage casings.

2. Grind the meat using a medium-course grinding plate

3. Fill the sausage casings firmly but not too tightly with the meat mixture.

4. Can be fried, grilled or barbecued over coals.

5. Makes 3.5 kg

Traditional Recipe for Dried Wors or boerewors

2 kg beef or venison (no pork or veal, it goes rancid when dried)

1 kg beef.

500 gr beef fat (no pork or bacon)

25 ml salt.

5 ml ground black pepper.

15 ml corriander, singed and ground (see hints and tips).

1 ml ground cloves.

2 ml nutmeg powder.

125 ml brown vinegar

200 gr narrow (thin) sausage casings.

Method

Cube all meat.

Mix together thoroughly and mince coarsely.

Place meat in large bowl.

Add all dry spices, and vinegar

Mix together lightly with a two pronged fork.

Place in fridge for +/- 2 hours to blend flavours.

Soak casings in water during this period.

Fit casings to sausage maker and fill with mixture.

Do not over- or under-stuff.

This wors is more suitable for drying than it is for cooking. Due to the absence of pork and spek, it is not as succulent as normal boerewors and many people find the cooked variety of this recipe a bit too dry for their liking.

Also, hang this wors a bit longer than other types of wors as most people prefer it drier than the rest. It should snap like a twig when bent.

Biltong

(Savoury Dried Meat)yet another essential snack for genuine south africans.

Once again, there are slight variations when it comes to ingredients, depending on personal preference.

12.5 kg venison or fillet, rump or sirloin

560 g fine salt

125 ml brown sugar

25 ml bicarbonate of soda

10 ml saltpetre (optional)

12.5 ml milled pepper

125 ml coarsely ground coriander

250 ml brown vinegar

2.5 litres warm water

Method

Cut the meat along the natural dividing lines of the muscles, down the length of the whole leg or a portion of it. Cut the pieces into strips 5-7 cm thick, with some fat on each strip.

Mix the salt, sugar, bicarbonate of soda, saltpetre, pepper and coriander together and rub the mixture into the strips of meat.. Layer the meat in a cool place for about 1 to 2 days, depending on how thick the meat is and how salty you want it to be.

Mix the vinegar and water and dip the biltong into it. Pat the pieces of meat dry and hang them up on S-shaped hooks - or use pieces of string - about 5 cm apart so that air can circulate freely in a cool dry place. Leave for 2 to 3 weeks until the biltong is dry.

Bunny Chow

A well known meal in Durban and KZn

Take 1/3rd loaf of bread and hollow it out. Then put whatever curry dish you have prepared in the hollowed out portion and garnish with some of the inside you have removed.

Rusks (Beskuit), a favourite for dunking in coffee

These rusks can be made from a variety of ingredients including: Aniseed, Buttermilk, All bran, Brown bread, and in fact any seads or nuts can be added.

2 cups unbleached white flour

2 cups whole wheat bread flour (coarsely ground if possible)

1/3 cup sugar

½ tsp salt

2 tsp baking powder

1 tsp cinnamon

½ cup melted butter

2 eggs

¾ cup buttermilk

2 tsp pure vanilla extract

2 tsp pure almond extract

Method

1. Preheat oven to 400 degrees. In a large mixing bowl, thoroughly mix the dry ingredients.

2. Combine all the wet ingredients, pour them into the dry ingredients, and stir until you have a soft dough, similar to biscuit dough.

3. Turn the dough onto a well-floured surface and roll or pat it to about a ½ inch thickness.

4. Cut the dough into rectangles about 2 by 4 inches. Bake the rusks about 2 inches apart on buttered baking sheet for about 25 minutes until the tops are crisping

and browning a little.

5. Now, eat a few "soft" rusks warm from the oven. Loosely pile the rusks on a baking sheet and keep them in a 200 degree oven all day or all night (about 12 hours) to dry.

6. The finished rusks should be very dry and hard. Cool and store in an airtight container. Rusks will keep for weeks.

Hertzog Cookies

500 g self raising flour

50 ml (4 tbs) sugar

25 ml (2 tbs) margarine

3 egg yolks milk or water

5 ml vanilla essence

1 ml (¼ tsp) salt

Filling:

Apricot jam

3 egg whites, stiffly beaten

250 ml (1 cup) sugar

500 ml (2 cups) desiccated coconut

Method

1. Cream the margarine and sugar in a bowl until light and creamy.

2. Stir in the egg yolks and vanilla essence, blending well.

3. Sift the flour and salt into the mixture, blending well, then stir in a little milk or water to form a fairly stiff

dough.

4. Roll the dough out to 5 mm thick on a floured surface and cut into rounds with a pastry cutter. Line greased patty tins with the rounds of pastry.

5. Make the filling. Gradually add the sugar to the beaten egg whites, beating well to blend.

6. Fold in the coconut and mix well.

7. Place a little apricot jam in the centre of the rounds in the patties and spoon some of the coconut mixture over the jam.

8. Bake in the oven at 200°C (400°F) until the pastry is lightly golden, about 15 minutes. Cook slightly in the patty tin, then cool completely on a wire rack.

Pap or putu porridge

This Mealie-meal dish goes under several names depending on the country.

It is also served as a side dish at barbecues and goes well with chakalaka

1 L (1¾ cups) water or water and milk combined

60 g (2 oz) butter

Salt to taste (optional)

500g (1 lb) corn (maize) or polenta

Method

Bring three-quarters of the water to the boil in a heavy-based saucepan which has a long handle for easier handling. Add the butter and salt. Put half the flour into a bowl, and add the remaining quarter of water. Using a wooden spoon, stir together to form a smooth, thick paste. Set aside. When the water in the saucepan has boiled, pour in the thick paste and stir quickly and firmly for about a minute. Bring the mixture to the boil. Gradually add the remaining flour and mix, stirring all the time, until it thickens sufficiently to form a stiff dough. Caution - this stage requires a lot of wrist power and firm stirring.

The consistency can be varied according to taste by adding more or less flour and/or water, When cooked, the pap should not stick to the side of the pan. Serve hot with meat stew and/or vegetables. Pap can be shaped into balls with an ice cream scoop and served surrounded by the meat and vegetables.

It is also a traditional side dish with a barbecue.

Pumpkin Fritters

4 c cooked mashed pumpkin

2 eggs

1 c flour

pinch of salt

1 teaspoon baking powder

30 ml (2 tablespoons) heaped of sugar

Method

Combine all ingredients, making a soft batter and fry spoonfulls in shallow oil till both sides are lightly browned. Drain on paper and serve warm with cinnamon sugar or caramel sauce.

Cinnamon Sugar:

Take one ounce of ground cinnamon and mix with 6 ounces of sugar. Sprinkle over pancakes as much as desired and keep rest in bottle for later use.

Peri Peri Marinade

The words Pili-Pili, Piri-Piri, and Peri-Peri all are used to refer to hot chile (chilli) peppers, sauces and marinades made from them, and foods cooked with those sauces and marinades. This spicy hot marinade can be used on any meat you grill or broil: chicken, beef, fish, seafood, etc.

Two or three fresh hot chilli peppers (red peppers are typical), chopped

Four tablespoons lemon juice or lime juice (or cider vinegar)

Four tablespoons oil

One tablespoon cayenne pepper or red pepper, or one tablespoon dried red pepper flakes

One tablespoon paprika

One teaspoon salt

One teaspoon minced garlic (or garlic powder)

Method

Combine all ingredients. Grind and mix the ingredients into a smooth paste. Adjust the ratio of cayenne pepper to paprika to taste. Rub marinade onto meat and allow to marinate in a glass bowl for at least thirty minutes before cooking. This works well on chicken, beef, or any other grilled meat.

Monkey Gland Sauce

Makes about 600 ml

2 medium onions, finely chopped

10 ml finely grated ginger root

3 cloves garlic, crushed

50 ml oil

125 ml each tomato purée and chutney

10 ml soy sauce

25 ml each prepared mustard and Worcester sauce

50 ml tomato sauce

75 ml port or muscadel

100 ml chicken stock, water or meat stock

30 ml red wine, vinegar or grape vinegar

salt and freshly ground black pepper

Method

Sauté the onions, ginger and garlic in the oil until the onions are translucent. Add the remaining ingredients and simmer over medium heat for 5 minutes. Serve hot.

Will keep in the refigerator for 2 weeks and in the freezer for 6 months.

Chakalaka

This spicy South African relish is an invention from the black townships and has become popular in the urban areas as well as a side dish at barbeques. The tinned version is now available in some supermarket around the world.

Preparing home made chakalaka is very much an individual thing, and depends on what you have available.

Here is a suggestion:

Chop tomatoes and onions to form the gravy, add garlic, chillies, and lots of grated carrot, some grated green or red pepper, and throw in baked beans. Cook till done

Green Bean and Potato Stew

500 g green beans, topped and tailed

1 potato, or more sliced

1 onion, sliced

5 ml salt

2 ml milled white pepper

100 ml water

2 ml freshly grated nutmeg (optional)

Method

Slice the beans into a saucepan. Add the potato, salt and pepper. Add the water and simmer the mixture, covered, for 30 to 40 minutes, or until cooked. Sprinkle with the grated nutmeg and serve as an accompaniment to meat dishes. The mixture can also be mashed and served.

Don pedro

Pour ice cream in to blender, and mix with liqueur of choice, add cream and blend before pouring into glass.

Acknowledgements

Grateful thanks to Catherine Murray from piggledesign. co.uk for formatting the book and her patience, understanding and belief in me, and "Penguin" Helen Courquin, the most special lady I have ever known, who gave me 10 years of happiness, and for taking the front cover picture.

Although every precaution has been taken in the preparation of this book, the publisher and author assume no responsibility for errors or omissions. Neither is any liability assumed for damages resulting from the use of this information contained herein.

Other books by the author John CT Miller include

Colour Blind a South African Memoir

This book tells the story of a young white boy growing up in Africa and how after he was blinded, went on to fight for his independence much like many of the peoples of Africa.

The book is at times humorous, at times insightful, and serves to remind the reader of the prevailing attitude of people and the government at the time, as well as a reflection of what apartheid was like in South Africa.

A Stage that Never Was

This is the story of a young innocent girl, who was in the wrong place at the wrong time and how after she